LAURA

the Unearthly

Burning Ember Press

This is a work of fiction. References to real people, events, establishments, organizations, or locales are intended only to provide authenticity, and are used fictitiously. All other characters, and all incidents and dialogue, are drawn from the author's imagination and are not to be construed as real.

A Burning Ember Book
Published in the United States by Burning Ember Press, an imprint of Lavabrook Publishing Group.

Cover design by Humble Nations
www.goonwrite.com

ISBN 978-0-9892064-2-6

For Dan,

Esto perpetua

Chapter 1

I WAS IN a burning house.

The oppressive heat evaporated the tears that ran down my cheeks, but my tiny hand still tried to swipe them away.

It was the sight of my small hand that made me lucid.

Not this again. Knowing it was a dream didn't stop the events from unfolding as they always had.

Smoke choked my lungs and obscured my vision. Which room was I in? I never could remember, no matter how many times the events played out.

Out of the smoke came a figure.

"Dad!" I yelled, my voice sweet and high-pitched.

He scooped me up as the wooden beams above us shuddered, and he led us through the smoky corridors. I watched from over my father's shoulder as fire ate up my house.

I blinked and a man stood amidst the flames.

My skin chilled despite the heat. *Not him.*

I gripped the expensive cloth of my father's suit and twisted it beneath my fingers.

The fire stung my eyes and I blinked. When I opened them again, the man was gone.

At some point my father stopped. The fire was not so bad here.

Another figure appeared out of the haze. Cecilia. I was passed over to her, out of my dad's arms.

"Dad?" I was scared again.

I hated this part.

He kissed me on the top of my head. "I love you angel." He turned away, disappearing into the smoke.

"Don't leave me!" I cried. But he was gone.

Cecilia led us through the house. I recognized my room along the way; my favorite teddy bear was lying on the floor, burning up before my eyes.

Cecilia carried me to our pantry. Barely glancing at the dried goods, she unlatched a trap door set into the floor. She dropped me down into the musty space before climbing down herself. I glanced back up through the trap door, wondering where my dad was.

She took my hand and led me through the darkness.

ꙮ ꙮ

"Reek! Reek! Reek!"

My eyes snapped open, and I sat up, startled. My heart was racing, and I shivered from the cold sweat covering my body. It took me a moment to realize it was my alarm clock that had shaken me from the dream.

I hit the snooze button and flipped over, rearranging myself to go back to bed. I was a good sleeper; even an old memory-turned-nightmare couldn't frighten me into wakefulness.

There was a knocking on my door. "Gabrielle, wake up!"

"No," I moaned.

"Time to get up," my mother said too cheerfully. "You're going to miss your flight if you don't get up!"

She walked into my room to assess the situation.

"But I just went to bed," I mumbled.

"That's what happens when you save packing until the night before your flight."

My eyes sprang open. Junior year. I had almost forgotten. I jumped out of bed and grabbed the clothes I had set aside.

"Breakfast is ready downstairs." With that, my mother turned and left.

I shoved myself into a black shirt, jeans, and a pair of boots. I popped into the bathroom and looked at myself in the mirror.

This was it. This was the last day I would officially live here. My nervous excitement had my adrenaline going. A year ago I'd never heard of Peel Academy, and now I was on my way to attend the prestigious boarding school.

ꕤ

I watched my mother's car pull away from the curbside, disappearing into the crowded airport traffic, and then I walked towards the airline check-in.

I fiddled with my luggage straps as I waited. Would I fit in? I desperately wanted to; it was part of the reason I'd accepted the offer of admission. God knew I hadn't fit in at my last school, or really any place for that matter. I clung to the opportunity to change that.

But there was a more important reason, one that I hadn't voiced to my adoptive mother. It wasn't that the school was located on the British Isles, and it wasn't that the school opened doors—though it did. It was a single line printed on the admission letter.

Considering your status as a legacy, Peel Academy warmly welcomes you into its esteemed halls.

Legacy. Meaning one or both of my biological parents might have attended Peel Academy in the past. This was my chance to find out who they were, and I was not going to turn it down.

I checked in and headed towards the security checkpoint. It was as I walked by the large panoramic windows that I felt my skin prickle and the back of my neck grow warm. Someone was watching me.

I scanned the bustling street on the other side of the glass, almost missing him. Nearly hidden by the shadow of the parking garage, a figure leaned against the wall.

Oh please, not *him*. Not now.

He wore a suit and a hat. For one brief moment we locked eyes. He tipped his hat. The seemingly innocent gesture sent a chill through me. I stood there in the airport and stared at the man, unable to look away. A Hertz rental bus finally broke the spell, its huge girth hiding him from view. I waited for the bus to pass. But once it did, the man had vanished.

My apparition.

I hadn't seen him in a while; I thought he was gone. But I should have known. The man in a suit was always there, since my earliest memories. Never changing, never aging, and always filling me with dread. I thought I'd be able to escape him by leaving, but maybe I was wrong.

ꕥ ꕥ

Eighteen hours, one layover, two coffees, and three bland meals later I arrived at Heathrow Airport. I could feel my eyelids drooping from lack of sleep, and my mouth felt gummy.

I still couldn't believe this was real. I got to live on my own and attend a private boarding school. The autonomy and adventure of it overshadowed the lingering sadness over leaving home.

I glanced around for my ride. I was supposed to meet Professor Blackmore at the baggage claim. As my gaze grazed over the various homemade signs, I felt a hand on my shoulder.

"Gabrielle Fiori?"

I turned and faced an older gentleman wearing a tweed coat, brown pants, and a red bowtie. A bowtie! All he needed was a monocle and a pipe to complete the look.

"Professor Blackmore?"

"Nice to meet you Gabrielle," he said, extending his hand. I shook it, relieved that I didn't have to scour the congested waiting area for my ride. "You were the last person we were waiting for. Why don't you grab your bags from the baggage claim, and then I'll go over our plans for the day."

Once I had collected my luggage, I joined the teens grouped together.

"Now that everyone on my list is here, welcome to the British Isles. As many of you probably know, we still have another leg of the journey ahead of us. I have a ticket for each of you—don't lose it—it's for our flight to the Isle of Man."

Shocked, I looked around me. No one had mentioned another flight. And where was the Isle of Man for that matter? The address on the school's website indicated that Peel Academy was in London.

Around me, students were smiling and happily whispering to one another. They definitely did not look surprised.

"Um, excuse me." I cleared my throat and stepped forward. "I didn't know we had another flight."

"Miss Fiori, it is customary for us to not publicly disclose the school's actual location before arrival," Professor Blackmore said.

"But what about the address on the school's website?"

Why the secrecy? I didn't say it out loud, but the shadowy way the school conducted business had bothered me. Not enough to dissuade me from enrolling, but enough to trouble me. Just accessing the website practically required fingerprinting.

Some of the other students glanced at me. Their looks clearly said I was an idiot.

"That address belongs to our London offices, where most of the school's official business and paperwork is processed." He faced the rest of the group, dismissing me. "Now, everyone, make sure you grab your boarding pass and follow me."

Had I missed a memo? No one else appeared to find this situation strange. And Professor Blackmore's answer only added to my growing unease. Reluctantly I took my boarding pass. My mother was going to freak when she found out. Oh well.

As we walked down the terminal, a student fell into step beside me. "I noticed earlier you sounded like you were American."

I glanced over at the girl next to me. She was curvy and had long golden hair that perfectly matched the color of her eyes.

"Yeah, I'm California grown," I replied. I noticed she also had an American accent. "You from the U.S.?"

She nodded. "I've bounced around a bit, but I'll always consider Boston home. I'm Leanne by the way."

"Gabrielle." Because she seemed willing to talk, I decided to ask, "Were we sent something that I didn't get? Because this is the first time I've even heard of the Isle of Man, and I seem to be the only one surprised by this."

"Nah, don't worry about it. Most of the students are legacies, so we already know the school's location. It's just not public knowledge."

I decided not to mention that I too was a legacy—there'd be too much backstory to cover.

"So you had a relative go here?" I asked.

"Yeah. My grandmother, and her grandmother before that."

"Dang." I was impressed. Some legacy.

I thought back to the dream I had so many hours ago. The memory-turned-nightmare was the last I had of my biological family. My mother back in California had adopted me as a little girl. Now I finally had the chance to find out more about my biological parents.

I couldn't wait.

ꕥ ꕥ

The flight took a little over an hour, during which I was able to get my hands on a map. The good news was that I was able to locate the Isle of Man. The bad news was that the map only depicted a meager dot between Ireland and Great Britain.

Fat lot of help that did me.

Once we landed, we were whisked to a car. We drove through a quaint town before the land opened up into rolling green hills sectioned off by squat stone walls.

Leanne pointed to little grassy lumps sprinkled across the landscape. "Those are ancient burial mounds; they've been around since the Bronze Age."

I tried to muster some form of appreciation, but they were a bit underwhelming to look at.

"And," she continued, unaware of my lack of interest, "our school is a castle."

"What?" Now that got my attention. The only images I'd seen of Peel had been either close ups, obscuring the building's façade, or indoor photos depicting the extravagant library and study halls.

"Yep. I didn't want to say anything earlier because it's technically a surprise, but everyone else already knows that Peel Academy is actually Peel Castle."

This was news to me. I got to attend class in a castle?

The school's website definitely didn't mention that.

The car rounded a bend, and the castle came into view. It was nestled at land's edge, perched atop coastal cliffs. Beyond it stretched the ocean. I sucked in a breath. Wow, that was where I got to go to school.

As we got closer, I began to notice some alarming details. There were no glass panes in the windows, part of the main building was crumbling, and one building didn't have a roof. What was going on?

The car passed through the gates, and we were on the school grounds.

I blinked in confusion. Stretching out to my right was a huge, sprawling castle. The windows were fitted with small, diamond panes and the roofs were immaculate. I blinked a few times. I must've imagined it, but I could've sworn ...

"Okay boys and girls, these buildings are the dormitories." Professor Blackmore pointed to our left. The car pulled up to a line of slightly more modern buildings that faced the castle grounds. "The men's dormitories are those just behind us, and the women's are these right in front of us.

Gentlemen, I am the house father, and ladies your house mother is Professor Nightingale. We live on the first floors of each respective dorm, and we are here to make sure you follow the rules and stay safe. Do not hesitate to come to us with any questions you may have. I have your room assignments and keys for the year. Don't lose them."

I collected my key and room assignment and hauled my bags out from the car. I first admired the castle before focusing on the dormitory buildings. I loved this place already.

I dragged my luggage past a reception desk where a security guard—a.k.a. a bored-looking college student—sat reading a magazine. When she saw me, she put the magazine down. "New student?" I nodded. "What's your name and room assignment?"

I looked down at my sheet of paper. "Gabrielle Fiori. Room 305."

She marked something off on a sheet next to me. "Nice to meet you Miss Fiori. Once you get your student ID, make sure to check in and out of here when you come and go. Your room's going to be on the third floor. Welcome to Peel."

I was sweating by the time I managed to drag my luggage up the three flights and find my room. Key in hand, I unlocked the door.

My dorm consisted of two twin beds, two desks, two armoires, and two closets all crammed into a tiny room. Despite the size, I couldn't complain, the view of the castle and the coast was that amazing.

I heard the door bang open behind me. Leanne stumbled in, dwarfed under all her baggage. "Stupid freaking luggage. Why did I think I could take all this with me?"

"We're roommates?" Thank goodness. I didn't know Leanne that well, but I liked her company and she seemed to like mine.

She looked up, her bags hopelessly twisted about her. "Thank all that is holy that you are my roommate. I was having nightmares that I'd have to live with Doris."

"Who's Doris?" I asked quizzically.

"The spawn of Satan," she said. "Unfortunately, you'll meet her soon enough. She's attending Peel as well."

Before I could respond, I heard a shriek from the hallway. A handsome guy with ice blond hair darted through our open door and tackle-hugged Leanne.

"It's *so* good to see you," he said, breaking away.

"How did you get in here?" she asked.

"I have my ways." He shrugged. "Oh," he said, noticing me for the first time. "Who is this beautiful creature?" he asked, walking forward. He eyed me up and down.

I blushed before I could help it.

"Stop freaking out my roommate," Leanne said. "Gabrielle, this is Oliver, my socially awkward friend."

"What's that phrase you Americans have?" Oliver snapped his fingers as it came to him. "Ah, I believe that's the pot calling the kettle black."

"Touché."

"So, ladies," Oliver said, "what are you wearing tonight for Mystique?"

Oliver walked over to one of the beds and made himself comfortable.

"What's Mystique?" I asked.

Oliver balked. "Don't tell me you haven't heard about Mystique."

I shook my head.

Leanne explained. "Mystique is a famous club on the island, and they host a party at the beginning of every school year to welcome the students."

"Let me tell you," Oliver said, "it's an event you don't want to miss."

Okay, a party. That could be fun. Instead my mind conjured up high school videos shown during Drug Free Week, filled with drunk high school students OD'ing on drugs.

"And," Leanne said, "let's not forget that Andre de Leon will be there."

"Who's Andre de Leon?" I was two steps behind everyone else. I swear I must have missed an email.

"She did not just say that," Oliver said.

Leanne shook her head. "Girl, you have a lot to catch up on."

"Apparently," I muttered.

"Andre de Leon is Europe's all-time bad boy," Leanne said. "He dates celebrities—and goes through them like potato chips—runs semi-legal establishments, and often gets in trouble with the law."

"You forgot the sexploits and the blood-drinking," Oliver said.

Blood drinking? What a disgusting fetish to have.

"I thought that fell under 'dating celebrities'?" Leanne said.

"Sure, whatever. Point is," Oliver said, facing me, "he's naughty and smoking hot, and he's going to be there tonight."

I smiled and tried to act excited about this Andre de Leon and tonight's festivities in spite of my stomach roiling. Call it intuition, but I had a bad feeling about the club.

Regardless, I would not sabotage my chances at friendship within the first day just because I didn't want to go.

A little dancing never hurt anyone.

Right?

Chapter 2

THAT EVENING, INSTEAD of walking out of the building, Leanne and Oliver led me down to the dorm's basement.

"Guys, I thought we were going to the party," I said.

"What do you think we're doing?" Oliver said. "Checking the plumbing?"

Leanne snickered. "You'll see." She pulled out her cell and turned on the phone's flashlight.

Spare mattresses leaned against a wall of the basement, and a few boxes sat to each side of the walkway. Directly above us was Professor Nightingale's room. I could hear her even footfalls as she moved back and forth across the room, pacing.

Further in, the room was filled with abandoned

furniture. Flush against the back wall was a bookshelf filled with dusty books. Oliver and Leanne approached it.

"It should be *Aesop's Fables*," Leanne said, pointing to a worn blue book. The gold lettering was barely legible. Oliver grabbed it and pulled. There was a groan as metal ground upon metal, and slowly the bookshelf swung open.

Above us the pacing stopped.

"Seriously?" I said. "This is our way out?"

"If you don't want to get caught," Oliver said, "then this is it."

"According to my grandmother, this passage should drop us off just outside the school. From there we can catch a taxi." I did the math. That was a dizzying distance spent walking in a cold, dark, underground passage.

"What is this?" I asked, eyeing the dark hole.

"A persecution tunnel. It's your medieval fire escape, although now mostly students use it."

Above us I heard Professor Nightingale's door open and close shut.

Oliver cursed.

"She's coming," Leanne said.

I bit my lip and eyed the dark tunnel. This was the time to make a new impression, a good impression, if I wanted to fit in. And I did, badly. While my brain was telling me to stay as far away from the creepy passage as possible, my ego was telling me that option was out of the question.

Outside the basement I could hear someone's footfalls coming down the stairs. Oliver and Leanne looked at me, eyes wide. I took a deep breath for courage, pulled out my phone, and flipped on my own flashlight. I walked ahead of Leanne and Oliver into the secret passage.

"I guess we'd better get going," I said. The damp clung to my tiny dress and I shivered. The cold had a hollow feel, as though there was not enough air to fill the dark passage.

Oliver whooped. "Someone's excited to par-tay!" he said as he entered the dark tunnel. Leanne followed close behind, making sure to shut the entrance behind her.

Maybe—just maybe—I'd make it here.

ꙮ ꙮ

I tugged down the short cocktail dress and took a sip of the bitter soda Leanne had bought me. We'd only been at Mystique for twenty minutes, and I was already regretting it.

"Ugh, it's so freaking humid! My hair is already starting to frizz!" Leanne shouted above the pounding music.

"Leanne, does your Coke taste funny? Mine does."

She gave me a look. "Of course it tastes funny. I ordered a Rum and Coke."

I choked on my drink. "But—but how could you? You're not eighteen," I stammered, trying to collect myself. I'd never had alcohol before. Considering its foul taste, I wasn't sure I liked it at all.

"I have a fake." My face must have shown my surprise because she rolled her eyes. "Listen, this is the only thing that will give me the courage to dance. And—" she eyed me up and down, "it will help you loosen up."

I huffed. I wasn't tense. Well, okay, I was extremely tense, but I was annoyed Leanne could tell. I took a healthy gulp of my drink; if the alcohol would help me relax, then I was open to it.

The place was packed with young, beautiful men and women. According to Oliver and Leanne, a majority of these people were my peers, out to enjoy the last bit of summer.

A sweaty Oliver bounded up to us. "Ladies, you need to dance! Put down those drinks." He tried to grab mine, but I resisted, clinging onto it for dear life. Now that I properly understood the perks of underage drinking, there was no way I was dancing without getting more liquid courage in me.

As we tussled for possession of the Rum and Coke, a hush fell over the crowd. I released the drink, only barely noticing as it sloshed on Oliver.

"Damnit Gabrielle, you could've given it up peacefully."

I felt a tingle up my spine, and I wondered if the

man in the suit had found me. Only the usual sensation was now slightly different. It felt ... *good*.

Then a second sensation hit me. Magnets. That was the best way to describe the pull. I was attracted towards something on the other end of the room, and it beckoned me to look up.

I let my eyes travel through the crowd, allowing the sensation to guide them. They found their target.

My gaze landed on a man's sculpted torso on the far side of the room. My eyes traveled upward, taking in his extraordinary height and his toned body barely hidden under his black button down. At last they reached his devastatingly beautiful face, framed by rich black hair. He had a strong jaw, sensuous lips, and dark, dangerous eyes.

Our gazes met for one perfect second, and the universe held its breath. Images flashed; nothing else existed. In that moment, I saw his past and my future. I saw a thousand images from an impossible number of lifetimes. And then I saw us. Together. *Always*.

The man's eyes showed surprise, and then wonder. And then the moment ended, and the world came rushing back to my senses.

I felt more than saw him take that first tentative step towards me. Adrenaline spiked my blood. I wasn't the curious type when it came to these situations. The man in the suit had fixed that years ago. After I got away, I'd think about what it all meant.

I slipped through the packed club, making my way

to the dance floor. After I'd crammed myself into the very middle of the mass of gyrating bodies, I glanced around for him. My eyes just barely caught sight of him.

He was casually scanning the crowd, which meant he had lost me. But just to be safe I pushed myself a little further into the sweaty mass of club-goers. I glanced back again, and he was gone.

Once I was sure I'd lost him, I moved through the crowd towards the back of the building. I needed someplace to be alone. Someplace where I didn't have to pretend to be having fun and where I could question my sanity. I came to a long hallway where the bathrooms and back entrance were located.

A sweaty blond man stumbled out of the men's bathroom. I tried to be as innocuous as possible, but out of my peripherals I saw him do a double take.

"Hey there," he catcalled. I could smell the alcohol on his breath from where I stood a few feet away.

I gave him a tight-lipped smile and continued walking.

"Where do you think you're going?" he asked. I continued walking. "Don't fucking ignore me." When I continued to do just that, I heard a shuffle of feet behind me and felt a meaty hand wrap around my arm.

"Let go of my arm," I said.

He laughed and pulled me closer. "What do I get out of that?" He pulled me in close, and I got a nearly lethal dose of his hot, putrid breath.

I probably should've given the guy some further warning, but I'd done this little dance too many times back in the States. I lifted my leg and stomped down on his foot with my heel.

He let out a howl of pain. "You bitch!"

Instead of letting me go, however, he pulled his hand back, preparing to give me a backhand slap. Before he had the chance to hit me, I kneed him in the crotch, silently thanking my mother for enrolling me in self-defense courses over the summer.

He crumpled to the ground, holding himself.

"Idiot," I said under my breath.

I began to walk towards the exit when I heard another voice behind me.

"Wait."

I turned as a shadow removed itself from the wall.

It stepped into the light, and my breath caught. It was the man from earlier this evening. The low lighting lit up his high cheekbones and strong jaw; it dipped and curved along his brow line. His dark eyes glittered as he moved. I'd never seen such a beautiful man before, or one that exuded such sex appeal.

"You know," he said conversationally, "assaulting a customer is prohibited in my club. Especially one as highly influential as him."

He walked closer and nudged the moaning heap on the ground. "However, he did have it coming to him." He smiled. "Andre," he said holding out his hand.

So this was Andre de Leon.

"Gabrielle," I said, not bothering to take his hand. "You watched the entire thing? And you did nothing to stop him?"

"I wanted to see how it played out. You seem like you can take care of yourself."

I huffed. "And you seem like you flatter people for a living."

He flashed me a grin that quickly turned devilish. "Okay Gabrielle, I'm feeling ... *nice* tonight. So I won't report this incident, and you can return to your friends—" I raised my eyebrows, "on one condition."

I paused and considered his words. "Thanks, but I don't think so."

"Pardon?" Now it was his turn to look skeptical.

"You heard me, *no*." I wasn't going to be blackmailed for a situation he could've prevented.

He scrutinized me. "Well aren't you just a feisty little thing," he said. I guess this didn't happen to him often.

"Are we done?"

"Come to dinner with me tomorrow."

I rolled my eyes. "You can't be serious?"

"Great," he said. "I'll pick you up at 7:00 p.m."

"Uh huh. Do you even know where I live?"

"Of course. You're a Peel student," he said as he began to move back towards the main area of the club. "And all of you live on campus."

I opened my mouth, but he cut me off. "And, to answer your next question, I know you're a student because I've never seen you before—and trust me, you don't have a forgettable face." He winked.

"Well, isn't someone a seasoned cradle-robber," I said.

He only smiled, the bastard. "See you Friday."

"I never agreed to the date!" I shouted after him, but he had already disappeared into the crowd.

ꟿ ꟿ

Almost as soon as I walked out of the hallway Leanne pounced on me. "Where have you been? I was really worried something had happened to you." She eyed our surroundings nervously.

"Something did happen to me," I said. "Andre cornered me in the hallway." Leanne's eyebrows shot up at the mention of Andre. "*And* he saw me knee a wealthy club patron in the crotch."

Leanne's eyebrows nudged up even further. Behind her Oliver extricated himself from the crowd and wandered over. "Hey ladies, stop being wallflowers and come join me on the dance floor."

Leanne ignored him. "So what happened after Andre saw all this?" she asked.

Oliver balked at the mention of Andre. "Whoa, what? You ran into Andre?"

I nodded. "He blackmailed me into going on a date with him."

"Wait—*WHAT?*" Leanne's eyes bulged.

"Oh my God! No way!" Oliver whooped. "You *go* girl! Way to make some *fine* lemonade out of lemons."

"Would you just shut up?" Leanne said. "This is *not* good."

"What do you mean *not good?*" He cocked his hip. "Andre's practically a god. Let Gabrielle be flattered—she just got asked out by an international celebrity."

"Yeah?" Leanne said. "Well, he's also a womanizer, and he has a criminal record a mile long."

"And has he gotten arrested yet? No."

I watched the two argue back-and-forth. It seemed useless to tell them I wasn't going on any date with Andre.

"That's only because everyone's too scared of him to do anything about it," Leanne replied.

"Or it's because his crimes aren't that severe. Just stop acting like going on a date with this guy is a fate worse than death."

"It could be," Leanne said darkly. Oliver just looked at her.

"Okay, okay guys," I said. "Let's just forget this whole conversation. I think I've had enough fun for one night."

ꕥ ꕥ

An hour later Leanne and I sat outside our dorm room, passing back and forth a thermos of coffee she had made. Oliver had already gone back to his dorm to get his beauty sleep.

"You know, you are so screwed now that Andre got you to go on this date."

I shrugged. "I'm not planning on going."

Leanne raised her eyebrows. "Andre is not exactly the kind of person that gets rejected."

"Well I'm not exactly the kind of person that gets blackmailed into a date."

She laughed. "Okay, it's your call. But this isn't going to end well."

Before I could answer, I heard voices in the stairwell across from us. "Did you see Andre de Leon checking me out?" The girl's voice echoed up the stairwell.

Next to me Leanne groaned. "That's the dreaded Doris," she said.

"If I stayed a little longer," Doris continued, "he might've invited me up to his VIP suite." Her friend murmured her agreement—I couldn't tell if she was being sincere or just trying to get Doris to shut up. How did anyone put up with that kind of narcissism?

Moments later two figures rounded the stairwell's corner and came within sight. One was a very beautiful, very drunk girl—judging by her staggering gait—and the other was a petite brunette.

"Seriously," Doris, the blonde, said, "If I hadn't left, it could've happened. Not that I would ever date a guy like Andre. Imagine what kinds of blood fetishes he must have." *Blood fetishes?* What was with this guy and blood?

Doris's unfocused eyes narrowed on us as she clumsily ascended the stairs.

"Have a fun night?" Leanne asked.

"Were you eavesdropping?" She directed her question specifically at Leanne, ignoring me.

"Kind of hard not to when you're shouting up a stairwell."

Doris tilted her head. "It must suck to know this is the closest you'll come to Andre, eavesdropping on a girl who actually has a chance with him." The insult wasn't aimed at me, but it didn't matter; I was offended.

I stood up and opened my mouth, about to defend my roommate, when Leanne cut me off. "Funny you should mention your chances with Andre," Leanne said, getting up, "seeing as how an hour ago Andre asked Gabrielle"—she motioned to me—"and *not* you on a date."

Doris's attention was suddenly, startlingly on me. Her eyes roved me over, head to toe, and then back up again, lingering on my face. The haughty set of her face flickered for a moment, and behind it I saw jealousy, intimidation, insecurity. I had that effect on some women.

And then the mask was back in place. Her lip curled. "I see Andre's standards have lowered." Her insult didn't sting. It didn't affect me at all. I shrugged, unfazed.

Leanne, who was busy relishing the moment stood up. "His standards still got a long ways to go before he'll look twice at you," Leanne said.

I raised my eyebrows. Leanne and Doris must've had some sort of history. This confrontation was too personal.

Doris turned on Leanne, leaning in close. "Just like you and Collin, right? Because that's what he told me after we made out—how unimpressive you were. Remind me, was that before or after you two broke up?"

Oh. No wonder the anger ran so deep. I saw Leanne's hands fist and knew this was going to get messy really quick. I eyed Doris's roommate, who was backing up down the hall. She was the smart one.

"Right, that was before you two broke up."

I saw Leanne's fist twitch, and I grabbed her as she lunged at Doris. Doris drunkenly staggered away, laughing. "You two deserve each other," she said, looking from me to Leanne with her unfocused gaze. "Losers."

Reflexively I loosened my grip, and Leanne nearly broke free. I grabbed her again as she began to slip away.

"Leanne, don't let it get to you. She isn't worth it." Despite how cliché the advice was, I meant it. My heart ached for my new friend, who had been betrayed by this venomous girl and an ex.

We watched Doris's retreating form. She was cocky

to have her back to us; if I were a lesser person, I would've let Leanne pulverize her.

"I hope she turns into a frog at the Awakening," Leanne spat.

I shook my head. "Leanne, what are you talking about?"

Leanne stared down the hallway even after they'd gone into their room, perhaps hoping Doris would walk back out. "Stupid nymph."

"Leanne, seriously, what's this about toads and nymphs and blood fetishes? And what's the Awakening?"

She reluctantly pulled her gaze away from the hall and looked at me. It took her a few seconds to react.

She cocked her head to the side. "Gabrielle, you don't know what the Awakening is."

"No, that's what I just said. Should I?" That's it. I must've missed an email. Of course this would happen. These things always happened to me.

Leanne let out her breath slowly, staring off into space. She nodded to herself, and then pulled out her phone.

"Hey Oliver, it's me. Meet me in my room. Gabrielle doesn't know what the Awakening is, and I'm not sure how to phrase it without totally freaking her out."

ᘓ ᘕ

We walked into my almost-unpacked room. Oliver pushed ahead of us and plopped himself down on my bed, managing to stretch his body out so that no one else could sit down.

"Really?" I looked at him.

"What?" He huffed and rolled his eyes. "Oh, don't get your panties in a bunch." He scooted over so there was enough room for me to sit. Barely.

"What about me?" Leanne demanded.

"My God, there's another bed three feet away," Oliver said to her.

"Move."

Under his breath he said, "I give an inch, and they take a mile."

Once we were all sitting, the room fell silent. For a few seconds Leanne stared at me. Seemingly lost, she glanced at Oliver. He shrugged his shoulders in response.

"Would you please just tell me?" I was getting uncomfortable with their silence.

"Listen Gabrielle, this is ... difficult to explain to someone who has not grown up knowing," Leanne said.

"Knowing what?"

"The truth about what we are."

"*What* we are?" The conversation was becoming cryptic.

"Oh, Leanne, you are doing a monstrous job of telling her."

My roommate gave Oliver a dark look. "Fine," she huffed, "you tell her."

Oliver took both my hands in his and looked me in the eye. "Honey, we are all supernaturals."

Chapter 3

"WHAT?" I COULD feel my eyebrows knitting together even as I smiled. I looked back and forth between Oliver and Leanne, waiting for them to tell me they were kidding. They looked serious. "What do you mean you're supernaturals? Tell me you guys are joking."

After a moment of tense silence, Leanne spoke quietly. "Of course we're serious Gabrielle. You don't get accepted into Peel unless you're a supernatural."

I raised my eyebrows, catching on to what she was implying. "So *I'm* a supernatural?" I couldn't believe I was actually entertaining the thought. "I mean, what even *is* a supernatural?"

"You'll find out what you are soon," she said hesitantly. "Your powers will surface at the Awakening."

"*That's what the Awakening is?*"

"Yes, and that's why only juniors and seniors attend Peel," Leanne said. "We've all reached puberty, and we're considered adults within the supernatural community; we're biologically and socially ready for our powers to be Awakened."

Her brow furrowed. "It's strange that you wouldn't know this. Everyone who attends Peel has usually known about his or her true nature since childhood."

"I was adopted at the age of five. Any ties I had to my biological parents were severed then." I didn't know why I said it. I wasn't entertaining these thoughts. Except that I couldn't help but consider it. Maybe that's why I saw the man in the suit. Maybe I *was* different.

Leanne and Oliver exchanged a troubled glance. I looked between them. The first seedling of belief sprouted. This wasn't the way two people would act if a joke went on for too long. In fact, it might explain why everyone knew more than I did. Or maybe I'd accidently joined a cult, and I was as crazy as everyone else.

"But how would the school know I was a legacy?" I asked. "I'm an orphan. Even I haven't been able to track any relatives, living or dead, and I've had over ten years to search."

"I don't know," Leanne said. "Someone must have informed them of your existence. But who?"

ꟹ ꟹ

I slept restlessly that night. The wind whistled outside my window, only adding to my nightmares. The man in the suit was at the back of my dreams, calculating. At some point the dreams dissipated, and I took comfort in the dreamless sleep.

I woke up to midday sunlight streaming through my window and a rapping on my door. For one blissful moment I lazily stretched my limbs, happy. Then I remembered the events of last night.

I briefly wondered whether I could actually be a supernatural. Impossible—but perhaps true. The thought, however, was soon eclipsed by another that had nagged me.

It was Leanne's final question that I couldn't get out of my mind. Did someone from my past know of my existence? Why hadn't they contacted me? Who were my parents, and where did I come from? These were all questions orphans asked themselves, but now answering them seemed vitally important. My future appeared to rely on it. I promised myself that as soon as I was settled in, I was going to do some sleuthing.

I heard the door open and a sassy voice chastise me. "Girl, get up! I know you are jet-lagged, but geez, it's almost 3:00 p.m. Even I don't sleep that late."

I sat up and rubbed my eyes. "Why can't you be like every other guy—hopelessly banned from the girl's dormitory?" I asked.

"Because I'm amazing." I felt Oliver remove my blanket and the pillow covering my face. "Now get your *ass* out of bed and get changed."

I groaned. "Why do you care?"

"I *care* because I don't want you to look like a homeless person tonight on your date."

"I'm not going." I threw my pillow at him.

He caught it and threw it back at me. "And I'm not leaving until you agree to come with me—unless you'd truly prefer to stick around and hang out with all the other *supernaturals*."

He had a point. "Okay, okay. Just give me five minutes to change."

I noticed Leanne was nowhere in sight; she had probably scrammed as soon as she could.

Oliver perched himself on my desk, arms folded.

"Let me clarify," I said. "Give me five minutes to get changed *privately*."

Letting out a melodramatic sigh, Oliver left the room.

I quickly threw on some clothes, brushed my teeth, and checked my reflection in the mirror. The blue-eyed, black-haired creature staring back at me looked wild and lovely. Sometimes I didn't recognize myself in her.

My gaze didn't linger long. I slipped on some sandals and headed out with Oliver to my version of hell—shopping.

ೞ ೲ

Four hours later Oliver came back with a pair of shoes and three shirts, and I came back with nothing but a full wallet.

Oliver threw his bags down and stomped over to Leanne's bed. For hours he had tried to get me to buy this or that revealing top, but he'd met his match. I was more stubborn than a mule, and proud of it.

Leanne came out from our room. "Hey," she said to me. She looked over at Oliver. "What's with you?"

He pointed a finger at me. "That one killed my shopping buzz."

I shrugged. "I'm broke. Plus, what's wrong with my clothes?"

Oliver raised his eyebrows. "Girl, are you for real? You need a new wardrobe like a werewolf needs a wax."

I rolled my eyes. "You've only known me two days, how could you possibly—"

Oliver pointed to my open closet and shuddered at the clothes sticking out. "The horror, the horror."

"Oh, get over it." I moved towards the door. "I'm going to pick up my schedule and some books."

"Oh, so *now* you want to spend money?"

"*Library* books. I'm going to pick up library books."

Leanne looked at me like I was crazy. "Aren't you supposed to be going on a hot date soon?" It was a quarter till seven.

"Yeah, that's not happening."

ꕥ ꕥ

I crossed the sprawling lawn that separated the dorms from Peel Castle with my student ID in hand, armed to pick up my class schedule and corresponding books.

I still couldn't decide whether everyone was seriously delusional, or if I had accidently entered into a cult. Either way, I was screwed.

The castle loomed in front of me. In the distance I could hear the crashing surf that surrounded the little outcropping Peel Castle was built upon.

According to the school map I'd been given, there were two libraries, but I was to pick up my books in the main one, which sat just to the left of the castle in an adjoining building. I opened the sturdy oak doors and walked inside.

Oil lamps burned soft and low. Couches and armchairs were placed between shelves of books, and a few sleepy-looking students lounged on these. Globes and busts of famous ancient thinkers sat on side tables, making the space feel less like a school library and more like an esteemed center for learning.

I breathed in the smell of musty books. It was one of my favorite smells in whole world.

This is surreal. I now lived on the British Isles, attended an elite boarding school, and had finally made friends. So what if those friends claimed we were all supernaturals? All other aspects of my life appeared to be equally surreal right now.

I walked up to the main desk and collected my class schedule and another sheet of paper. On it was a list of books. "Can I pick these up right now?" I asked.

"Sorry hun," the librarian said. "Today seniors are picking up their books, so if you want your books now, you're going to have to hunt through the shelves to find them."

"Sure—thanks. That shouldn't be too difficult."

The librarian raised an eyebrow and gave me a Mona Lisa smile. That couldn't be good.

Walking away, I skimmed the book list. The first title caught my eye: *Introduction to Monsters.*

Wait. What?

ꕥ ꕥ

At precisely seven o'clock, a sleek black Mercedes pulled in front of the women's dormitory. Clad in a suit and holding a single red rose, Andre stepped out of the car. His curling brown hair brushed his collar, and he moved a loose strand off his forehead.

It had been a surprisingly long time since he was last here, but nothing had changed. A young woman sat behind the front desk in the lobby, reading a magazine. She looked up in time to see him heading for the stairs.

"Uh, sir, excuse me, you need to sign in before I can let you upstairs. ..." Her voice died when she saw who it was.

"Of course." Andre walked to the desk and signed the blue sheet of paper.

He smiled charmingly. "A 'Gabrielle' lives here, and I am supposed to meet her tonight. Would you know what room she lives in?"

"Sure," she said nonchalantly, but her hands were shaking. She was probably breaking the rules by giving him this information—by letting him in at all—but she wouldn't stand up to him, almost no one in the world would.

The woman scrambled through some loose papers on her desk. "Gabrielle Fiori? She lives in room 305."

He felt his composure slip a little. "Did you say Gabrielle *Fiori?*"

Santiago's daughter.

But that couldn't be. She died in a fire long ago. How was she still alive?

"Yes. Is something the matter?"

He composed himself. "Not at all. Have a lovely evening." He gave her a wink, and went to the stairs. She giggled nervously behind him.

Gabrielle Fiori ... interesting.

ꟾ ꟾ

Andre knocked on the door of room 305.

"Geez Gabrielle," the girl said as she opened the door, "you don't need to—"

The door opened, and a girl stared at Andre with

a mortified expression. Gabrielle was definitely not in the room.

He hid his displeasure with a smile. "You must be Gabrielle's roommate." He held out his hand. "Andre."

She eyed his hand like one might a poisonous snake. Slowly he let it fall.

"Do you know where Gabrielle is?"

He could see the girl's breath quicken. She was nervous. Good. "Sh—she's at the library picking up her books."

The library. He strode down the hall, leaving her stuttering for words.

A minute later the dorm's front doors burst open, and Andre stormed out. As Andre left the building, he threw the rose into the trash.

His driver got out of the car. "Sir?"

"Take me to the campus library."

ꕤ ꕤ

Peel's library was close to the dorms, and the car ride was short. Yet it was still plenty of time for Andre to seethe. When was the last time he was stood up? He couldn't even remember.

The Mercedes came to a halt, and for a second time that evening Andre stepped out. Now, however, all traces of his suave manner were gone. He was pissed.

He walked up to the library's thick oak doors and

kicked them open. They slammed against the wall, the wood splintering apart.

Startled students screamed at the noise. More joined in once they saw who was standing at the library's threshold. Andre scanned the crowd, looking for one person.

Gabrielle.

His eyes found her as she walked away from the counter, forcing books into an already overstuffed bag. Belatedly she noticed the silence. She looked around until she caught sight of Andre.

"Shit," he heard her swear under her breath.

Chapter 4

WHY HAD HE come looking for me? Couldn't he take a hint?

Andre angrily stalked forward until he was more than comfortably close. In a deceptively calm voice, he asked, "Did you forget we had a date tonight?"

Silence. Everyone was in the library was listening.

I lifted my chin. "A 'date' would suggest mutual interest. What you did was blackmail."

For a moment, nothing happened. Andre just stood there frozen, as though he had not registered my words. Then, before I could react, he picked me up and threw me over his shoulder.

"What the—? Put me down, now!" Instead of putting me down, Andre began walking to the door, like any normal caveman. Students who had gawked at the scene now parted to make room for him. No one was going to do anything. In fact, they all looked a little frightened.

"Help! Please, someone! Andre, put me down!" I began to bang on his back with my fists and my book bag. I tried to wiggle off of him, but he had a viselike grip on me.

Now I began to scream. "Help!"

Andre pushed open the doors, and the night's chill rushed over my skin. He didn't stop walking until he came to a black Mercedes.

A man came out of the driver's seat. "Sir?" He sounded concerned.

"Everything's fine. Could you grab the door? Oh, and turn on the child lock."

The man hurried to open the rear car door. I huffed. Andre was kidnapping me, and his driver opened the door for him?

Andre unceremoniously dumped me into the car and followed me in.

I scrambled for the far door. Grabbing the handle, I pulled. Nothing. I tried again.

"Damnit!" Fruitlessly I pulled on the handle a few more times, but nothing. I wanted to cry.

The driver got in, and the car pulled away from the curb.

"Sir, are we still going to the marina?"

There was a long pause, long enough to make me

look over at Andre. He was assessing me with his eyes. "Yes, I think that would be best." I attempted to put as much distance as I could between him and myself, leaving me squished into the corner of the car.

I sputtered, "You're still taking me on the date? Are you kidding me? You can't just snatch me up and—"

Midsentence Andre turned his attention to my books, which had miraculously made it into the car with me. In particular, he focused on a textbook that had slid partially out of the bag.

"*Living and Dying in a World of Wonder: An Introduction to Supernatural Beings*," he read out loud. I let out an indignant huff and crossed my arms. "They're still making students read this?" He pulled the book out of my bag and began flipping through it. "You know, this book is nearly as old as me," Andre said.

I eyed the book, a cloth-bound, gold-leafed book that looked like it came straight out of Old Man Time's library, and then looked at Andre, who appeared to be in his mid to late twenties.

"That book is nearly as old as you? That's a joke, right?"

My words irked Andre; his eyes narrowed. "It's a manner of speaking."

"How old *are* you?" I asked. It was a rude question, but I had a right to know how old this guy was if I was being forced on a "date" with him.

"A little over seven hundred."

Now I was thoroughly confused. "Seven hundred ...

years old? Wait. What? You're actually serious?" All that is holy, please tell me I was not trapped in a car with a crazy person.

Andre's mouth quirked as his irritation turned into wry humor. "You haven't heard? I'm a vampire."

ꕥ ꕥ

"The man who wrote this textbook was a classicist. He ranked beings on a spectrum from good to evil."

I was still reeling. A vampire? Either Andre was crazy, or he was telling the truth and he ate his dates. There was no good way to look at it.

"Hmmm ..." He was preoccupied flipping through the pages. "'Vampires: nocturnal, blood-drinking beings who, in exchange for their mortal life and immortal souls, are granted theoretically eternal lives, as they can only die from suicide or murder. Vampires are unequivocally the most evil creatures who once began life human.' Well I'd say that's a bit harsh."

"I think it's appropriate considering you've kidnapped me and will probably eat me and throw my remains into the water."

"I do not 'eat' people," Andre said. "And if I wanted you dead, I have far more practical ways of accomplishing that."

Great. He just admitted he offed people.

He began paging through my textbook once more. "Oh, here's your entry. 'Sirens: grumpy birdlike creatures who badger men to their deaths with their incessant squawking.'"

"Give me back my book!" I tried to make a grab for it, but he moved it out of my reach.

"Ah," he said, focusing his sharp eyes on me, all playfulness gone, "so you were fine ignoring our date, but now you're not fine when your wishes are ignored?"

"I never agreed to the date. And how would you know whether I'm a siren?"

He gave me a once over. "I guessed. Sirens always were so annoying."

I was a siren? Something else about his sentence caught my attention. "Sirens *were* annoying? Why the past tense?"

There was a moment of silence before he spoke. "They tend to live very short lives."

I swallowed. That was a bad omen, especially now that I was trapped in a car with a vampire.

"And of course you agreed to the date," Andre added.

"I did not! And while we're on the subject, why don't you apologize for carrying me against my will to your car—and for blackmailing me."

"I will do no such thing. I would do it again if circumstances were similar."

I wanted to scream. This man was unbelievably frustrating.

"Look," I said, exasperated, "I'm assuming people

kiss your ass for a living. And I'm assuming you come from a time when it might've been perfectly okay to throw an uncooperative woman over your shoulder. But, if you want to have any chance with me, then you have to give me some reason to respect you."

I wasn't planning on any future dates with Andre, but I could scrape up my pride with an apology.

Andre looked like he bit into something sour.

"Sorry," he said flatly. It wasn't an apology. Not even close.

I felt the car slow down before coming to a complete stop.

The driver opened my door—which I noticed was unlocked from the outside—and let me out.

I shivered as I stepped into the cold night air. The chilly wind brought goosebumps to my skin. I looked around. We were amongst rows and rows of docked boats.

Suddenly, Andre was there next to me, putting his coat around my shoulders.

I stepped away from him and let the coat slide off. It crumpled into a pile on the damp dock.

I looked down at it. "Sorry. I hope your coat wasn't too expensive," I said as I read the Armani label on the inside.

He laughed. *Laughed.* What was it going to take for this guy to drive me home?

He picked up the crumpled coat. "Fine Gabrielle. You don't want the coat? We'll see how cold you get before you ask for it back."

ꕥ ꕥ

How cold was it? Really effing cold. I sat shivering on one of the damp vinyl seats as Andre steered the boat. Of course, my being on the boat was the result of a series of events that culminated with me sitting on the dock, refusing to step onto the boat. Surprise, surprise, Andre dealt with the situation by picking me up—again—and carrying me onboard.

Now we were giving each other the silent treatment. And under no circumstances would I break that silence to beg for the coat. Even though I couldn't feel my nose. Or my hands.

In spite of the frigid evening, I was able to enjoy the view. The castle was luminous. Strategically placed lights made the old stone walls glow a yellow orange. The city of Peel was no more than a cluster of lights along the dark landscape, becoming more infrequent as we moved away from the town.

As I stared out at the lights, I felt the heavy weight of a blanket placed on me. I looked up at Andre and, through chattering teeth, said, "Thanks."

I wrapped the thick blanket around me, beyond caring that I was ever so briefly nice to him.

Eventually Andre turned the boat around and we docked. I ran ahead of him to the car and asked the driver to crank up the heat, where I sat—blanket and all—and allowed myself to defrost.

Andre got into the car a little while later, brooding. I guess most of his dates usually played out better than this. I bet he even thought I'd stay the night in the boat's little cabin with him. Ha!

"James, take us back to Gabrielle's home."

We sat there in tense silence before he finally spoke. "So I guess that didn't go as planned."

"I think you owe the library money for the doors."

"It's already taken care of," he said.

I took that in. "That was quick. I guess. Whatever."

And those were the last words I spoke to Andre. I thanked the driver for the ride when he pulled up to my place. Grabbing my book bag, I scrammed. It was only as I entered my dorm room that I realized I still clutched Andre's blanket to my chest.

ꕤ ꕤ

"I am so sorry," Leanne said before I could even shut the door behind me. "He was really scary. And he intimidated me. Kind of."

I sighed. I now knew and had seen enough about Andre to understand that Leanne didn't have much choice. The guy was pretty efficient at getting what he wanted.

"Don't sweat it." I walked over to my bed and dropped my stuff down next to it.

"I'm just glad you're okay. I heard about the library.

Someone filmed it and posted it on the Internet."

I put my head in my hand. This couldn't be happening.

"Oh my Lord, is that who I think it is?" Oliver called from the doorway. "How was your date? I saw the video. So hot. I bet he was so hard to resist."

I turned, letting him take in my blue lips and unpleasant expression. "Andre is a prick."

"Honey, what happened?"

I curled up on my bed and recounted my date to both of them, beginning with the library and ending with the awkward drive home.

Oliver fondly patted my knee. "He was definitely after your virgin treasure."

Leanne nodded. "You dodged a bullet. Anything with Andre tends to end badly."

I figured that, of course. But in spite of the terrible date, and Andre's questionable motives, later that night, I fell asleep clutching his blanket and breathing in the ocean and him.

Chapter 5

AT 6:00 P.M. the next evening, Oliver, Leanne, and I, along with the rest of the new juniors, gathered on the grass outside Peel Castle.

Tables and chairs dotted the lawn between the dorms, and candles glowed from each table's centerpiece. All set up in preparation for our Awakening.

An older woman ushered the three of us to a table. Immediately after sitting, my foot began to jiggle. Curious by nature, I couldn't tell if I was more nervous or excited for the evening's events.

Fifteen minutes later, the murmuring of anxious voices quieted as an older gentleman walked up to a makeshift podium on the far side of the lawn. He tapped the microphone a few times, and then his voice boomed over loudspeakers.

"Good evening." He had everyone's attention. "For those of you who do not know, I am Archibald Hazard. Welcome to Peel.

"You are here because each and every one of you is intensely exceptional." His eyes moved over the crowd. "You have come from all over the world. Some of you are in the entertainment industry. Others have competed in the Olympics or made critical advances in science. And a few of you have been touched by great tragedy." His eyes briefly rested on mine.

"But all of you are truly exceptional for a different reason. I'm sure at some point in your lives people thought of you as strange. Abnormal."

His words struck a chord.

"Perhaps it was an ability to foretell events. Perhaps it was extraordinary strength or unusual beauty. Perhaps it was a powerful love of the forest, or a bone-chilling fear of fire.

"These are your birthrights. You are the result of generations of magic passed down across millennia. Tonight we will give you the opportunity to finally embrace your heritage. Tonight, we welcome you into our community and recognize you as a member.

"However, during this time of excitement, it is important to remember that you were chosen because we saw true and honorable characteristics in each of you. Empathy. Fairness. Sacrifice. Not all people born with your gifts are allowed to Awaken them."

Leanne leaned in to me. "Then how was Doris not screened out?" she whispered. I bit back a laugh.

"Many of you come from schools where breathing incorrectly earns you a detention. You will not find that to be the case here. In the supernatural world, sixteen has always been the age of adulthood. The members of Peel Academy uphold this long-standing tradition and recognize your autonomy and maturity. As a reflection of that, we expect you to make wise choices as the young adults you are."

I was considered an adult? The thought of legal freedom, which I hadn't thought would come around for another two years, was intoxicating.

"While you will find few rules here, those rules that remain are taken very seriously. Danger is real, and we respond severely to any misuse of power.

"Remember that tonight we bestow on you all a great privilege and a great burden. Never forget that these new abilities of yours come with the expectation that they will be used to promote good and keep evil at bay.

"Congratulations on your great accomplishments, and I look forward to meeting each and every one of you. Enjoy your evening."

Applause thundered from the crowd as we stood and clapped. And in that moment, I felt like I might actually be one of them. I might actually fit in.

After the speech, dinner was served. I barely touched my food. No one seemed to know what was going to happen tonight.

By the time our plates were taken away, the sky was a deep blue, and the lamplight illuminated our faces.

Professor Blackmore walked onto the podium, clad in what must be his usual tweed suit and bowtie. "Ladies and gentlemen, the moment has come. Men, please meet your patriarchs at the north end of campus. Women, please meet your matriarchs at the south. Let the Awakening commence."

A solemn silence descended as the students were beckoned into separate clusters. Leanne and I followed the crowd to the south, where the "matriarchs" of the group then led us by torchlight—yes, torchlight—into the castle.

We passed through several stone halls lined with old tapestries and coats of armor. The path descended downwards, underground, through a twisting maze of chambers. Eventually we were ushered into a room.

It looked like a gentleman's library. The room was spacious, filled with several couches. Books lined the walls. Low burning oil lamps sat perched on small tables. Here and there were marble busts of the Greek gods, miniature ships in glass bottles, a few globes, and several large Greek vases.

I thought it was pretty trusting of the school to put over a hundred excited women in a room full of breakable objects—but that was just my opinion.

Once we were all in the room, one of the matriarchs who hovered near the door cleared her voice. "Ladies, tonight marks the first night of the rest of your life. The women around you will become some of the most important people in your life. Take this time to get to know one another. As for tonight's events, each of you will see us in a little while. Until then, good evening." She inclined her head.

Those matriarchs who'd been standing in the room filed out. Once they'd exited, the woman at the door backed out of the room, closing the door with a firm click.

The sound echoed throughout the room. All was silent for a moment.

And then the moment was broken.

"What is going to happen to us?"

"How long are we going to be here?"

One woman tried the door. "The door's locked. They locked us in!"

ꕥ ꕥ

We didn't hear from the matriarchs for an entire hour. When we finally did, a knock on the door interrupted our conversations. The door opened, and a severe-looking woman came in.

"Daisy McFallon!" she called out.

Murmurs blossomed throughout the room.

The girl standing next to me hugged her arms. She looked wide-eyed around at the rest of us. I guess this was Daisy.

"I'm sure everything's fine," I reassured her.

She nodded once to herself and took a deep breath. "That's me," she said, her voice carrying above the others.

"Please come with me," the woman said.

The room had fallen silent, the crowd of girls parting like the Red Sea to let Daisy through. No one wanted to associate themself with her in case they'd get called away as well.

Slowly, reluctantly, Daisy walked to the door. The woman whispered something to her, and they both left. Once the door clicked closed again, the room let out a collective breath.

I thought I was right, that everything was fine. But I was wrong. Daisy never came back.

Chapter 6

In fact, the room slowly and innocuously began to thin out. Panic returned as girls were quietly ushered out of the room. Some cried when they heard their names called, frightened of the unknown.

"Leanne Summers!" the woman at the door called.

Leanne gave my hand a squeeze. "I guess I'll see you on the other side."

I gave her a tight-lipped smile and watched her leave, wondering if and when I would get called.

I didn't have to wait long. The next time the woman came back, it was for me.

ꟈ ꟈ

"Gabrielle Fiori!"

I maneuvered my way around the several dozen women who still remained and over to the woman at the door.

She leaned in. "Follow me."

She grabbed a torch from its post outside the room and led me down the hallway.

My heart fluttered as the torchlight played across my chilled arms. My overactive imagination could've sworn the subterranean air felt thick—as though it were holding its breath.

Although the passage didn't appear to slope downward, I had the impression we were walking even deeper underground. The stone walls on either side of us were damp with perspiration, and somewhere in the distance I could hear a dripping noise. Every now and then a torch mounted on the walls lit the dank hallway, giving off a little flickering light.

We stopped in front of a thick wooden door that looked like it led to a dungeon.

The woman turned to me. "There is a white robe in the room. Take off all clothes but your undergarments and put it on. Leave the rest of your items—including your shoes—in the room. I will come back once you've changed, and we'll continue."

She walked away, along with her torch, throwing me into near darkness.

"Oh, no big deal. I'll just get naked in this dungeon," I said under my breath. I walked into the room, which was little more than a fancy closet. Someone had draped a white robe over a red velvet chair. Next to it sat a vanity and an antique mirror. A tiny candelabra and an oil lamp provided the only light.

The door clicked shut behind me. Out of curiosity I tried the handle. Locked.

I shook my head. This was freaking weird.

I quickly changed. The robe was a gossamer, floor-length shift. Gold rope hung from the shoulders. I crisscrossed the rope between my breasts and tied it at my back. Looking in the mirror, my reflection bore an uncanny resemblance to a sacrificial virgin.

The soft glow had turned my skin golden and dilated my pupils. I looked every bit as mystical as the rest of Peel, and for a second time this evening I let myself hope that I might actually belong here.

My thoughts were interrupted by a knock on the door. "Are you ready?"

I gave my reflection one last look.

"Yes."

The unnamed woman opened the door and once again took me down a maze of halls. The darkness was disorienting, and I couldn't be sure whether we had walked this passage before.

Then we turned down a hallway I *knew* we had never passed through. Hundreds of gaping human skulls lined the walls, many warped from moisture and time. Water dripped from their grotesque grins, and I had the distinct impression they were laughing at me.

In the middle of the hall we stopped. "You are now

about to enter the most secret of our chambers," the woman whispered. "Until Awoken, visitors are not allowed to see the last of the passage."

This didn't bode well—the most secret room was just beyond the hall of horrors.

She continued. "To keep the chamber secret, and to respect the sacred space, I will have to blindfold you."

"You'll have to *what?*" I did not whisper, and my voice echoed down the corridor.

"I will have to blindfold you," she repeated, looking annoyed.

I crossed my arms. "Why should I trust you?" I asked. I was literally in death's alley, about to experience a ritual I knew nothing about with people I knew nothing about, and now they wanted to blindfold me?

The matriarch laid a hand on my shoulder. "No one is forcing you to make this decision. You can leave. We are not a cult, and we do not want you to think you have no choice in the matter. That being said, you must wear the blindfold, or leave."

What she hadn't said was that if I left, I'd have to drop out. Only the Awoken attended Peel.

I took a moment to consider her words. I was against this creepy, ritualized activity. But she was wrong. I didn't have a choice. This school was the only link to my past. Going to school here would bring me closer to figuring out who my parents were and what had happened to them. It would give me closure. I wanted—no, *needed*—to find that out.

I rubbed my eyes. "Okay," I relented. "You can blindfold me."

The blindfold slipped over my eyes. The matriarch then took my hand and led me forward.

It took forever to get to our destination, but at some point we stopped. I heard the woman knock on a door, and, after a moment, the sound of groaning hinges. She led me forward into the room.

I could hear chanting all around me. The beautiful harmony danced along my skin, drawing out goose flesh. Inside myself, I felt something loosen and stir inside, reacting to the pull of the words.

Abruptly, the song ended, and the blindfold was taken off.

The first things I noticed were the candles. There had to be hundreds of them, scattered throughout the cavernous room. I noticed that many of them were clustered around a human shaped alter. I swallowed.

The women in the room wore silken robes in colors that ranged from gold, to burnt umber, to scarlet, to plum. Perhaps it was the lighting, but they appeared to glow, and the air in between us sparkled, as though it were heavy with something.

Out of the crowd a woman came forward. "Welcome Gabrielle Fiori, daughter of Celeste." I physically started at the name. Were they talking about my biological mother? I quickly shrugged off my excitement. Celeste was probably someone associated with the ritual. Still, I made a point of remembering the name.

The matriarch took my hand and led me into the group of women. They gathered around me, some touching my hair, others my robe.

"You are here, daughter, sister, mother, because you are a link in the great chain of extraordinary women. Do you accept your heritage?"

Silence. I cleared my throat. "Um, yes."

"Very well."

A goblet of some sort changed hands.

"Gabrielle Fiori, we have chosen you. You are exceptional, not only for being a product of your forefathers and mothers, but also for your inner strength, empathetic nature, and honorable character.

"Join our ranks. These walls have centuries of women's names etched into them." And heads. These walls had centuries of women's heads. They forgot to mention that. I guess once you joined, you never left.

"Allow us to Awaken your birthright, handed down to you by your noble ancestors."

A woman holding the goblet stepped forward. She held the goblet out to me. "I, Anastasia, offer you the wine of the enchanted. Drink and Awaken."

She extended the goblet to me. For a moment, I could do nothing. The phrase "don't drink the Kool-Aid" came to mind. But I wanted answers.

I took the goblet and drank from it. The substance was rich and cloying. It had to be laced with something, but the dominant flavor was irresistible, and I couldn't stop drinking. Without consciously realizing it, I had finished the goblet.

I blinked a few times. Why had I finished off the entire glass?

The goblet slipped from my hands. Distantly I heard it clatter on the ground. Someone took my hand and led me forward. I looked at her. The contours of her silhouette were indistinct; they reached out from her like rays, then retracted, expanding and contracting to the pounding of my heart. The chanting began again, and the women moved, becoming bright blurs.

The light from the candles flickered like a silver screen projection, one moment blindingly bright, the next moment dim and dark. The room tilted slightly.

I tried to focus on individual women, but my eyes wouldn't adjust. I stumbled a little, but someone was there to catch me. It was hard to walk; I couldn't feel anything. My eyelids closed, and I let myself fade away.

ꟸ ꟸ

The girl began to fall as the wine took effect. The matriarchs nearest her caught her slumbering form and together arranged her on the altar. This was where the true magic began.

They joined hands, and the chanting increased in volume. The witches in the room focused the magic, coaxing it from the depths of the unconscious girl.

Slowly, it blossomed, taking on a golden hue and illuminating the girl from within. It concentrated in the bloodstream before moving outward, towards the skin's surface.

The moment the magic broke through the surface, the girl's skin rippled. A thousand feathers—or maybe they were scales—ruffled along her skin before resettling. Invisible once again.

"We welcome you, siren," a matriarch proclaimed.

But the magic was still thrumming through the girl. She had more to Awaken. Golden particles coalesced over the girl's heart. They thinned and stretched upwards, creating a fine golden cord.

"A soulmate," someone breathed.

"We welcome you, soulmate," another matriarch proclaimed.

The golden cord receded into the girl's heart. Still the magic would not settle.

"Strange indeed," someone murmured.

A sudden gust of wind tore through the cavernous room, blowing out the candles and torches. Someone screamed.

Something evil had entered, but the matriarchs knew not what presence joined them. The only light source was the girl's magic.

The matriarchs waited, holding their breath.

Suddenly the girl's body began to convulse. Her back arched. There were more screams as women ran to her.

Blood oozed from the girl's eyes and ears, and her lips pulled back. The matriarchs watched as two long, sharp canines extended themselves. Blood dripped from her teeth as her gums ripped.

As quick as the convulsions came on, they ended. The girl's body dropped back onto the altar, limp like a doll. The magic receded back into her.

"Let's get some light in here," a woman said.

A few candles were lit, and the matriarchs slowly approached the girl. A brave woman put her fingers to the girl's neck.

After a moment she turned to the others. "Call an ambulance!"

ᘓ ᘐ

I woke up to darkness. I blinked in an effort to make out my surroundings, but I could not see anything. As I tried to sit up my head hit a solid surface.

"Ow." I reached up to rub my head, and my elbow banged against a metal wall, making a tinny, reverberating sound.

I tried not to panic. *Where was I?*

I tentatively reached up and touched the low metal ceiling. It felt flimsy. My hands followed the ceiling's contours and quickly hit the edge of what appeared to be a metal box.

I felt around with my feet as my pulse spiked, now frantic to figure out where I was. As I moved, a piece of paper attached to my big toe brushed my skin. I sucked in my breath.

Oh. No.

I remembered from CourtTV. There was only one place where tags were placed on toes. The morgue. Somehow I had ended up in the morgue.

I let loose a bloodcurdling scream and began kicking the metal wall beyond my feet. To my shock, as I kicked the wall, the metal gave in. It groaned as each successive blow dented it outwards.

On the other side of the metal I heard someone cursing.

"Help! Please!" I shouted.

I heard someone swear. "What in the world—"

Suddenly I was rolled out from my metal prison. I sat up, belatedly realizing that only a thin paper blanket covered me. I clutched it to myself and squinted up at a young man in scrubs. His face was pale and his eyes were huge as he stared at my lively appearance.

He began to back up. "I-I'll go get ..." He turned on his foot and sprinted out of the morgue.

I sat there, stunned by my surroundings. Had I—*died?* I tried to recall my last memories. I remembered wearing the white robe and being led into a dark room. Women dressed in shimmering garments gave me something to drink. Then it all went fuzzy.

For a moment that was all I could recall. Then a dizzying series of images came flooding back. There had been blood everywhere—and the awful convulsions. I put a hand to my mouth when I remembered the sharp, lacerating pain where my gums split open.

What had happened to me?

Distantly I heard a series of footsteps slapping against the linoleum along with the sound of rickety wheels.

The doors burst open, and a group of doctors and nurses came in, wheeling in a gurney. They placed me on it and began strapping various medical instruments to my body. Then the questions began.

"How long have you been awake?"

"Five minutes?"

"Are you experiencing nausea?"

"No."

"Does anything hurt?"

"Not particularly."

"How do you feel?"

I thought about this last question as they rolled me down the hall.

"I feel good." I paused. "Actually, I feel really good."

In fact, my senses were sharper than they'd ever been. I could see clearly all the way down the hall. And I could smell everything, from the chemical scent of disinfectant, to the underlying smell of bodily fluids—sweat, vomit, urine, blood.

I asked aloud the question that plagued me. "Why was I in the morgue?"

The doctor nearest me looked over. "Last night you were proclaimed legally dead."

Chapter 7

All the tests indicated that nothing was wrong. My death and later resuscitation were inexplicable.

I lay for hours in the hospital bed as doctors monitored my vitals and analyzed my blood work. It was only once I tipped them off about my excellent eyesight and sense of smell that weird results began to appear.

I was able to read the entire eye chart down a hundred foot hallway. I could hear conversations through closed doors. I could pick up emotions by scent. And I had gained immense physical strength, as the mangled drawer in the morgue illustrated.

Even with this information, doctors had no idea what I was. Correction, *supernatural* doctors had no idea what I was. There was no name for what I had become, and no one had ever heard of a student Awakening only to die. So again, they put me in a hospital bed while they began analyzing my test results.

I was imagining shapes in the abstract wallpaper when there was a knock on my door. A doctor came in, followed by Professor Blackmore and a middle-aged woman in a conservative business suit.

The doctor addressed me. "Gabrielle, you probably know Dr. Blackmore." I nodded, smiling at the quirky professor. He gave me a smile and a wink. "He's been researching your case since it was reported last night. After your results were inconclusive, he suggested we use ulterior means to figure out what you are.

"This is Madame Levine," the doctor said, introducing the woman. "She is a seer, and we brought her in to look into your future. We think she might be able to shed some light on what happened to you and what was Awakened in you last night."

A seer? Someone was going to look into my future? This was beyond strange. Then again, compared to how I spent the last twenty-four hours ...

Madame Levine came over and sat on the edge of my bed. "Have you ever had a reading?" I shook my head. "I'm going to take your hand to establish a connection," she told me. "Then I will look into your future to see if we can figure out what you are. This should take no more than a minute or two."

Gently she picked up my hand and closed her eyes.

She sat still for about ten seconds, and then her eyes darted back and forth beneath her closed lids.

She squeezed my hand as though something surprised her. With my improved hearing I noticed the moment her breath hitched and her heart rate increased.

Her lips moved and she attempted to speak. I leaned in to hear her better. "Unnatural," she mumbled.

Suddenly she began thrashing her head back and forth. The doctor, Professor Blackmore, and I looked at each other, not sure whether this was normal.

With a final gasp she dropped my hand, rubbing her own as though I had burned her. She backed away from me, fear in her eyes.

"Abomination." She pointed at me. "Vampire! The devil has marked you, and he will claim you."

Vampire? But I thought I was a siren.

I was taken aback by the rapid personality change. A minute ago Madame Levine was sweetly walking me through her divination process. Now all she needed was a torch and pitchfork to complete the image of the fearful villager.

Madame Levine turned to the doctor and Professor Blackmore. "She has only a couple years to live. Then she will die again and awake as a vampire. The change is already beginning."

I could smell the fear rolling off of her; the scent excited me. I felt every inch the monster.

She backed out of the door, never turning her back

to me. Her brisk footfalls echoed down the hall, and I felt an alarming urge to chase her.

Professor Blackmore stared at me, curious. "I have never heard of a vampire being Awoken." He rubbed his chin. "Then again, I have never even heard of a vampire being *born*."

He turned to the doctor. "You know what this means. You must call *him*."

The doctor's eyes widened. "No Geoffrey, I can't make that call. The man is a monster; he is not allowed in my hospital."

Professor Blackmore addressed him. "She needs to be formally introduced to the clan she is now a part of, before she becomes a potential menace to humans."

Ouch.

The doctor was shaking his head.

"In addition," Blackmore continued, "she could become the target of violence. The relationship between the mainstream supernatural community and vampires is strained enough. She needs the support of her own clan. Not to mention that the vampires might also perceive her as a threat if they do not understand what she is."

"Geoffrey, do you understand what exposing her—"

"Make the call—or I will." Professor Blackmore's sharp tone did what his reasoning couldn't.

"Fine," my doctor said. "Against my better judgment I'll do it. I just hope this is the right choice."

With that, he left the room.

Dr. Blackmore walked over to my bedside and sat down in a guest chair. "Are you all right?"

"I think so," I said. But I wasn't all right, not by a long shot.

"Have you been able to contact your family?"

"No." A rebellious tear escaped. I was not going to feel bad for myself. I took a deep breath. "It's just me and my mother—and she adopted me, so I'm not sure she would understand my ... situation."

My mother. I'd give anything to talk to her. I was alone and scared; that's when mothers are the best. But she wouldn't understand. She'd think I'd gone crazy and pull me from Peel. And then I'd lose the only opportunity I'd ever had to figure out who my biological parents were and how I came to be adopted.

Professor Blackmore smiled sympathetically. "I'm sorry to hear that. Most of the students have family to get them through this. Has anyone here informed you of what happened between your Awakening and the morgue?"

"No." I hadn't even thought to ask. "To be honest, I didn't know there was more to tell." I'd become a pseudo-vampire, a revelation they'd seemed as baffled about as I was. I figured that was all there was to know.

"Well then, it falls to me to help you fill in the blanks."

I let out the breath I didn't know I was holding. "Thanks."

He gave me a tight-lipped smile. "When you drank the elixir, it Awoke your dormant supernatural traits. Three traits surfaced—"

"Three? You mean I can have more than one supernatural ability?"

"Oh, of course," Professor Blackmore said. "Some traits are compatible with others. Three is a bit rare, but far less unusual than being born a vampire." He smiled at me and patted my knee. "You happen to also be a siren and a soulmate."

I wasn't too surprised to find out I was a siren, but I had no idea what that last one meant. "What's a soulmate?"

Professor Blackmore chuckled. "It's exactly what you might think it is. You have a single true love out there. Only in the supernatural world, it means your soul is inextricably bound to him or her; it's a physiological, psychological, and spiritual connection."

I looked at him skeptically. "You've got to be kidding me."

"I take it this is good news?" he asked.

"Good news? There are seven billion people out there, and I'm only compatible with one? No way. Those are the worst odds ever."

My outburst brought on a fit of husky laughter. It took Blackmore a couple minutes to cough and regain his composure, but the twinkle in his eyes never went away. "That's a very astute observation. Our community tends to believe being a soulmate is romantic."

I sniffled a little. "Man, it's been only bad news for the last twenty-four hours."

The sweet old man patted my hand. "Good and bad things have a way of evening themselves out. I'm sure your bad luck will not last forever."

I was mulling over his words when a wave of raw power washed over me.

"Do you feel that?" I asked Professor Blackmore.

"What exactly are you feeling?" His tone reverted back to one of scholarly curiosity.

I sat up a little straighter and stared at the door; the sensation came from somewhere beyond it. Power flowed over my skin, building on itself as its source came closer. The rush made me feel giddy.

I glanced at Professor Blackmore. I could tell by his expression he still hadn't noticed the surge of energy.

I heard a doctor shouting down the hall. "You are not authorized to be here!"

Suddenly, a familiar form filled up the doorway. "Hello Gabrielle."

Professor Blackmore had been wrong. My bad luck was only just beginning.

Chapter 8

"*THIS* IS WHO you had the doctor call?"

Andre. I tried not show how shaken I was by the surge of power that accompanied him. It was there still, thrumming like background noise—very *loud* background noise.

However, unlike me, Andre seemed unfazed by the situation.

"Do you two already know each other?" Professor Blackmore asked.

"Unfortunately," I said under my breath.

Andre sauntered in, assessing the small hospital room then drinking me in with his eyes. "So," he crossed his arms and leaned casually against the door, "you're becoming a vampire?"

"Apparently," I said. Of course we couldn't just part ways after our bad date.

"Well then, we need to introduce you to the coven and begin training."

"Training?"

"To control your new powers. We don't want you—how did you put it the other night? Oh, *eating any of your future dates*."

Oh no.

It sank in then. I was becoming a vampire, and Andre was a vampire. We were both going to be kicking around for a long time, and now that we were part of the same clan, I had a sneaking suspicion that we were going to see each other. A lot.

So much for going our separate ways. Life really screws you sometimes.

ഗ ര

Andre had called an emergency meeting for any vampires in the area. I was to be introduced in an hour. On the way to the meeting, we made a pit stop at my dorm so I could take a shower and change.

When we arrived, the woman manning the desk did a double take as Andre strolled in behind me.

"Miss, guest hours end at 9:00 p.m. I'm sorry, but your friend has to ..." She trailed off as she took me in. "You're that girl—they said you died."

"I didn't," I replied. "I became a vampire."

She gasped at my words and made the sign of the cross.

Call it a sore spot, but her reaction ticked me off. "This is what you have to deal with every day?" I asked Andre. He raised an eyebrow. "No wonder you have anger management problems; you've had to deal with these people for centuries."

"I do not have anger management problems."

The woman's eyes darted back and forth between me an Andre, wild and frightened. I could smell her fear, and it sent a shiver down my spine. I felt Andre's hand on my shoulder. The touch brought on a zing of electricity.

Pull it together. He didn't say it, but the gesture did.

"Can my ride please come up? We are on a tight schedule. I have to meet my clan—"

"Coven," Andre corrected.

"Excuse me, *coven* in less than an hour, and I need to get ready."

She was shaking her head vigorously back and forth—which I took for *yes.* I grabbed Andre's hand and, ignoring the zing of energy and the live current now circulating between us, led him to my room.

My place was empty when I arrived, something I was exceedingly grateful for. It would be difficult to explain to Oliver and Leanne everything that had happened to me and still make the meeting on time.

I felt Andre behind me; the thrum of his energy stretched and receded like a rubber band when we were near. He walked over to my bed and picked up his blanket, his expression smug.

He lifted one of those deliciously sculpted eyebrows. “I think someone likes me.”

I snatched the blanket from his hands. “Don’t get too excited. I was cold.” I was also a liar, and he knew it.

His look became heated, and he smiled suggestively. God help me, I was getting turned on. He began walking towards me, and that electric charge between us surged.

He came in close and stopped. Not meaning to, I breathed the scent of him in and shivered. He was turned on—I don’t know how my nose detected it, but I could tell. This smell thing was freaking me out.

He leaned in, his breath tickling my skin. “I think we have some unfinished business. I think you *do* like me, and I’m prepared to convince you until you can no longer deny it.”

The air thickened, and my breathing came out in ragged bursts. Something was going on between us, and if I didn’t end this soon, I was going to do something regrettable.

I stepped around Andre and grabbed my towel and some clothes from my closet, breaking our connection. I walked to the door and turned back to him. “Convince away.”

ᘓ ᘐ

I took a quick shower, dried my hair, and threw on my clothes. When I walked back into my room Andre was sprawled out on my bed, holding a framed picture of my mom and me at one of my old track meets.

"This is your adoptive mother?"

"Yes."

"She seems nice."

"She is." I crossed the room and took the photo from him, placing it back on my desk. It unnerved me to have him peering into my personal life. Only then did I notice what he said.

I froze. "How did you know I was adopted?"

He shrugged, but a smile tugged at the corner of his lips and his eyes glittered mischievously. "I can tell you, but it will cost you."

"It will cost me what?" I asked, agitated.

Now his smile widened, showing pearly white teeth and a little fang.

We both heard my heart rate pick up at his unspoken offer. "Are you seriously going to withhold my family's past from me?" I asked, exasperated at the entire situation.

His eyes twinkled.

Yes, he would withhold the information I desperately craved.

I shook my head. I could expect no less from the same man who thought it was okay to kidnap an uncooperative girl for a date.

I grabbed a coat from my closet and tugged it on.

"Ready?"

He got up slowly, slinking towards me. The energy between us pounded in my ears and swept across my skin. Then he passed me, and the energy ebbed.

"I'll take that as a *yes*."

We walked down the stairs. In the lobby the girl behind the desk was speaking on the phone and biting her nail anxiously. I still hadn't seen Professor Nightingale since moving in, and it appeared that she couldn't be bothered for this kind of problem. So much for having a house mother.

When the girl behind the desk saw us, she pulled the phone away from her ear. "Is your friend leaving?"

"We both are," I said.

"Students are not allowed to leave—"

"Just call Professor Blackmore. He'll okay it," I said, not breaking stride.

"You can't lea—" The doors closed behind us, muffling her protests.

"Okay, so where's this meeting happening?" I asked.

"My place."

"You're taking me to your *house*?"

"I'm not exactly thrilled to bring you there, so stop staring at me like I'm going to deflower you." He had the audacity to look martyred. As though he hadn't been propositioning me only minutes ago.

"My house functions similarly to Buckingham palace—I both work and relax there."

"Oh."

We walked towards his car, some exotic sports model that had to be worth more than what most people made in a year.

"Consider yourself lucky," he added. "Many would die for the opportunity."

I was mid eye-roll when I caught his wording. "Die? You don't actually kill anyone, do you?"

He opened the passenger door for me. His chivalry didn't fool me. The man had already thrown me over his shoulder—twice.

"No—well, not usually. Only on my off days."

"*What?*"

"I'm kidding," he said. "Has anyone told you you're no fun?"

"I'm so much fun." I sounded whiny, even to myself. "Has anyone told you that you are difficult to get along with?"

He smiled, showing some fang. "Many. It's part of the job description."

༄ ༄

"Before we arrive at Bishopcourt, there's something I want to show you," Andre said, his eyes never leaving the road.

I raised my eyebrows. "I have to be honest with you Andre, I think I've had enough surprises to last me a long time."

"I promise you'll like this one."

We drove for about ten minutes, just long enough to hit the outskirts of the city, before Andre pulled over to the side of the road. "Close your eyes," Andre commanded.

"Nuh uh. Last time I did that I woke up in the morgue."

Andre sighed loudly. "Fine. Let's get out."

"Where are we going?"

"Are you always this stubborn?" he asked, rubbing his jaw. I tried to not concentrate on how sexy the action was.

"Are you always this rude?" We stared at each other for a few moments before he turned and began jogging away from me.

"Where are you going?" I called after him.

He didn't respond. I contemplated just standing there and seeing what he would do if I didn't follow him, but curiosity won out. I jogged up to him.

"About time," Andre said as I ran alongside him. "Come on, let's pick up the pace."

Andre took off. He should have been a blur, but my new eyesight was able to follow him easily.

"What are you waiting for?" he called back to me.

I blinked. Oh—I could run fast now. I picked up my pace, building my speed up. The fields I ran through flew by, gradually becoming denser and transitioning into forest.

I could no longer see Andre, but I could sense him ahead of me. A minute later I felt Andre stop. I ran towards him, his energy my lodestone. I heard the sound of running water seconds before I came to a halt next to him.

"This is what I wanted to show you," Andre said, extending a hand to encompass the grotto.

I looked around me and gasped. How had I not noticed it before? My supernatural eyesight added an entirely new depth to the night. All living things produced a subtle glow, brightening the dark. It was luminous, and I watched, mesmerized.

The pool of water in front of us glowed as fish swam underneath its surface. In the trees I noticed owls, their bodies shining brighter than the surrounding plants.

"This is ... *beautiful.*"

Andre smiled as he stared about him. "I often forget what it's like to experience this all for the first time." He looked over at me. "I'm glad I got to be the one to show you."

"How come I hadn't noticed this earlier?"

"The city is too bright for us to pick up this type of light."

We stood there for a long time, just watching this secret little world.

Eventually Andre glanced at his watch and broke the silence. "Let's get going. It's time to introduce you to the coven."

ഌ ഋ

As we approached a high security gate, I considered the course my life had taken. Less than a week ago I had no idea the supernatural world actually existed. Now, not only was I a part of that world, I'd also managed to become an outcast. I found it ironic; I'd been so skeptical of their world that I hadn't considered they'd be skeptical of mine.

We rolled up to a wrought iron gate, and a security guard sitting in a nearby booth nodded to Andre. The gate swung open and the car rumbled through. We sped along the road for another few minutes before we approached a grand mansion. According to Andre, this was Bishopcourt, his estate.

Andre broke the silence. "The doctor said you died at your Awakening." I met his eyes. He looked concerned. It was difficult to dislike him when he acted like he cared.

I broke eye contact and stared out the window, taking in the group of people waiting for Andre in front of his mansion. "Did they tell you I woke up in the morgue?"

"Yes." I expected him to laugh, but instead his voice was solemn. I turned back to him. His eyes were searching my face, and I got the impression he was memorizing something about me.

Reluctantly he broke his gaze and turned off the car. As soon as the ignition was off, Andre's minions descended on us.

"Good evening miss," said the man who opened

my door.

"Evening," I murmured back. This was so strange.

I looked over at Andre, who was exchanging formalities with one of his people. He was a chameleon; all signs of his somber mood had vanished the instant he left the car. He caught my stare and smiled. The sight of his smile sent a jolt through me.

Breaking away from the small crowd that had formed around him, he came over to me and wrapped an arm around my shoulders, sending a shock of energy through me. "Don't look so freaked out. We haven't even gotten to the good stuff yet," he whispered into my ear.

I discreetly shrugged his arm off, and together we walked towards the mansion.

The two guards who stood to either side of the doorway bowed in unison and opened the door for us. My jaw slackened, and I did a double take of Andre, sure I had missed something. The guy was a celebrity; I expected the attention. But bowing? That indicated reverence.

"Who are you?" I asked.

"I am the king of vampires."

Chapter 9

I STOPPED WALKING. I'd never felt more out of my element. "You're a king? And these people are what, your minions?" I gestured to the great number people who appeared to be waiting on him.

"They are my subjects," he said.

I let that sink in. An undead king. No wonder the guy couldn't take no for an answer.

We walked down a long hallway, turned down another, and finally stopped in front of a pair of closed doors.

Andre placed a hand on my shoulder. "Before we go in, I should mention that the audience might be hostile."

I doubled back to glare at him. "What do you mean

'hostile'?" I squeaked.

He heaved a tired sigh. "No one's going to hurt you Gabrielle. You are one of us. It's just that no vampire has been created in almost a century—and no vampire has *ever* been born."

"No no no no no," I said, shaking my head. This was too much. Having to face a coven—a freaking *coven*—was strange enough. But a potentially *hostile* group of vampires? I'd get eaten alive—literally. I began backing away.

Andre saw the mutiny in my eyes. "Oh no you don't." He reached out to grab me, but I was too quick. I bolted.

I ran back down the hallway we came through, amazed at how swift I had become. The gold leaf molding that decorated the hallway blurred.

Andre was not pursuing me, but then he didn't have to. From my peripherals I saw a blur of movement, and I had less than a second to react before a huge body tackled me. The air in my lungs whooshed out as I landed hard on the ground. But as quickly as I was knocked down, I was dragged up again.

I looked up at my attacker's face, and all I saw was fang.

I let out a surprised scream.

"Thought you'd get away, eh?" the man asked in a thick Scottish accent. He held my upper arm and walked us back down the hallway. I struggled against him for a bit, but my new powers had no special effect on him. Defeated, I allowed him to lead me back. Andre waited by the double doors, arms crossed.

"I'm guessing this wee one is our guest of honor," my attacker said.

"She is." Andre inclined his head. "Thank you Theodore."

Roughly, Theodore let me go, and I stumbled forward. Andre caught me and turned me around.

"Gabrielle, meet Theodore, my second-in-command."

I eyed the man who tackled me; I disliked him immediately. "You owe me an apology."

He looked amused.

"No," Andre said, "he doesn't. You ran away like a fugitive and Theodore caught you. Now stop wasting time."

I gave Andre my best stink eye. "God you are rude. No wonder you go through women. One hour with you, and they are probably begging to leave."

Theodore laughed. "Oh, I really like her."

Andre frowned, but whatever he was going to say was interrupted as the double doors in front of us opened.

"Ready?" he asked, reaching for my hand.

I ignored the gesture and walked through the doors.

ꟗ ꟗ

"I have gathered you all together for a very strange and

important meeting—" Andre spoke to the beautiful, undead crowd.

My hands were clasped tightly together, my knuckles white.

"—to meet our newest member."

The crowd collectively gasped, and I saw a few vampires literally hiss in response.

Someone spoke up. "But it is forbidden to create a vampire!"

Another voice joined the first. "Who did this to her? Have they been punished?"

"She smells human!"

Suddenly the room was full of angry voices.

"Quiet!" Andre's voice rang out above the others.

The crowd fell silent and he continued. "Her name is Gabrielle *Fiori*."

This started another round of excited chatter.

Andre put a hand up. "Yes," he continued, "the same Gabrielle who was thought to have died in the fire that killed our dear friend and comrade."

My eyebrows rose. He knew about the fire? I thought his statement had shocked me, until he spoke again.

"Gabrielle died two nights ago during her Awakening and was reborn this way. You see, no one changed Gabrielle. She is the first and only vampire ever to be born. She is the biological daughter of our late friend, the vampire formally known as Santiago Fiori."

ꙮ ꙮ

Santiago Fiori. My father. How had I ever forgotten? His name kept running through my mind; I wanted to burn it into my memory so I'd never lose it again.

"See, that wasn't so bad," Andre said as he walked me back to his car.

I rolled my eyes. "Yeah, such a friendly reception. I especially liked the comment about how tasty I smelled."

I was trying for sarcastic but fell short, still distracted by all this new information. I wanted to ask Andre more about my father, but he had already proven himself to be the manipulative type. I would have to find the answers I sought some other way.

Andre casually reached out and took my hand, and I brusquely pulled my hand away. I knew it was rude, so sue me. I held grudges, and Andre had a whole bag full of them.

Andre was unfazed. Tenacious vampire.

"You know that being part of the coven means you will always have our protection. My protection," he said. "You will also always have a home here. We look out for our own. Don't think that because the others were taken aback by you tonight that they don't like you."

I didn't respond to his statement, but it reminded me that no one had mentioned anything about a siren or soulmate clan.

We got in the car and Andre pulled away from the mansion.

"Hey Andre?" I said. He glanced over at me. "Do sirens and soulmates have a clan gatherings?"

He slammed on the brakes. I grabbed the holy shit handle as my body was thrown forward.

"Geez! What was that for?" I asked.

"What did you say?" Andre's voice was lethally quiet, and the hair on my forearms rose in response.

"I wanted to know if sirens and soulmates had clan gatherings."

"Why?" His voice was hostile.

I gave him a look. "Why do you think? I happen to be both."

"You're a soulmate." His eyes were deep and searching.

"Yes," I replied slowly. "That's what I just said."

He turned back to the steering wheel, thinking.

"So ..." I continued, "do either sirens or soulmates have a clan I need to visit?"

"No." He wouldn't look at me. "Soulmates are not a recognized clan, and you are the last of the sirens." I raised my eyebrows at that.

All sirens die young. I guess I was no exception.

ꙮ ꙮ

The car ride was quiet while Andre brooded. It was only as we entered the city of Peel that he broke the silence.

He pulled a business card out of his jacket's inner

pocket. "This has my contact information. Don't hesitate to call if you have any questions about your ... transition. All fledgling vampires have mentors. Mentors used to be those vampires who were responsible for the change, but since creating vampires was outlawed and since your circumstances are unusual anyway, consider me your new mentor."

"Oh goody." One failed date, an Awakening, a death, and a rebirth later, and now Andre was my mentor.

"Let's meet up tomorrow evening so I can begin to train you."

"Why is turning someone into a vampire not allowed anyway?"

He took his time answering and chose his words carefully. "Because the devil owns all vampires' souls. And at some point, we realized this and cauterized our acts."

Perfect.

Andre drove past the security gates and onto campus grounds, and I remembered the trouble we ran into when we left Peel Academy earlier that evening.

"Aren't you going to get into trouble for being on campus?"

His lip quirked, and he snickered to himself. "Cute question."

"Oh really?" I asked, annoyed.

He glanced over. "Trust me, no one's going to cross me."

The car pulled up to my building, and I opened the door and got out.

"Gabrielle."

"Yeah?" I turned back to look at him.

"Be careful." His eyes looked worried.

"Don't worry," I replied, "I'm resilient."

"I wasn't talking about you."

I swallowed and closed the car door, watching him as he drove off, his engine echoing along the empty streets even after the car vanished from sight.

ᘓ ᘐ

I stood there for a long time afterwards, my thoughts far away.

My skin prickled, and the hair on the back of my neck rose. I put a fisted hand to my mouth, muffling my rising scream.

He was here. The man in the suit. I could sense him before I saw him.

I looked down the cobbled street and there he stood under a streetlamp.

I nearly stumbled from shock. He had almost always sought discretion when he appeared before me. Now, his obvious presence felt more menacing than before, as though he no longer feared making contact with me.

I stayed still, staring at him. To run seemed foolish. I couldn't hide from him.

He spoke to me, his words tickling my skin as though he stood right next to me.

"Hello Gabrielle." The man inclined his head in greeting. "I have waited a long time for this night."

I met his terrible gaze. "What do you want?" I whispered.

"You."

Chapter 10

"WHY?" I RECOILED at the thought.

He just smiled. "... Although it appeared that I almost lost you a couple nights ago. Heinous thing death is. Luckily, you've now cheated it." His gaze never wavered, and even from the distance his eyes were deep and dreadful, hiding all sorts of unpleasant secrets.

"How did you know that?" My voice shook, and any semblance of bravery crumbled.

"I'll be watching you Gabrielle."

He winked, and his form was blown away by a fierce wind that tore at my hair.

I rubbed my tingling ear, wanting to wipe away the closeness of his words. They felt too much like a lover's caress. My hands trembled, and I took a few deep breaths to calm myself.

It was strange walking back into my building. A different woman sat at the security desk, and she didn't bat an eyelash when I walked in and signed my name on the activity log, even though it was late.

I could really get used to this newfound autonomy the school offered.

When I stepped onto my floor, I had the misfortune of running into Doris, who was her usual catty self.

She looked me up and down. "Are you a zombie now, or a bloodsucker?"

I ignored her, and kept walking to my door.

I heard her call to my back. "I hope you know that everyone thinks you're a sorry freak."

My ability to put up with crap was spent after the evening's events. That, at least, was the only excuse I had for what I did next.

I turned, quicker than her eyes could follow, and was on Doris in an instant. I pushed her against the wall, and it pleased me to hear her pathetic whimper. My reflexes were now quicker than my emotion, and it was only after I had pinned her that I felt some dark, primordial excitement pulse through me.

I made eye contact with her, and whatever she saw in them made her flinch. I could feel my anger growing, feeding on itself.

"You're right Doris." I spoke low so only she could

hear me. "I am a freak. But I'm also a predator, and you, Doris, are most definitely prey. Just remember that next time you want to pick a fight."

I let her go and watched her stumble away to her roommate, who stood at end of the hallway. I took a few deep breaths, trying to reign in my uncharacteristic anger.

Doris glanced back at me to shoot me a glare, but it was her roommate's expression that haunted me. She looked at me like I was a monster. Worst of all, I believed it myself.

❧ ☙

"My love! You're all right!" Oliver squeezed me against his nonexistent bosom, showering me with affection I ill-deserved. "We thought you were dead!"

He and Leanne had decorated our dorm with balloons and a "Get Well" sign. I guess they ran out of "Glad You Didn't Die" and "Please Don't Eat Me" banners at the drugstore. But it was incredibly sweet, even if I still felt like a complete schmuck for scaring Doris. I'd sat in the stairwell for a good fifteen minutes before I mustered the courage to face my new friends.

Leanne came up to me and squeezed my hand. "She deserved it," she said.

I must've looked shocked because Leanne laughed and said, "I'm a seer. And I totally foresaw that fight go down about three hours ago, much to my excitement."

When I didn't laugh, she added in, "Sorry."

I shook my head. "It's okay. It's not your fault at all. I'm just a little overwhelmed with everything that's happened since the Awakening." She nodded sympathetically. "Aren't you guys freaked out that I'm going to become a vampire?"

Oliver began to laugh hysterically. "Seriously Gabrielle? Look who you're talking to—I'm a gay fairy. I'm the world's biggest cliché. It's not like we get to choose these things. Besides, fairies are also 'evil' according to that stupid textbook of ours."

"And I know a good person when I *see* one," Leanne said, snickering at her own joke. "Get it?"

"Please, Leanne," Oliver said. "Just stop it with the seer jokes. You're beating a dead horse, only this poor horse died hours—"

I grabbed my friends and went in for a group hug. "You guys are amazing."

"Duh," Oliver said. "As if you hadn't figured that out by now."

꧁ ꧂

The next morning my alarm clock went off. I groaned, rubbing my temples. I'd stayed up way too late.

"No," Leanne moaned. She had too.

"Tell me about it," I muttered.

An hour later the two of us stumbled outside. Oliver leaned against our building's wall. "What took you broads so long?"

I gave him the stink eye.

"Ah. You two didn't get your beauty sleep. ... Well, let's get going. Don't want to be late on our first day."

The Isle of Man decided it was going to be sunny today, an unusual occurrence. The sun was painfully bright, making my eyes tear up. Stupid vampire genes.

We crossed campus and entered the castle. Around us, teens were hurrying off to class. I pulled out my schedule.

Period 1: Science and Magic
Period 2: Supernatural Combat
Period 3: History of the Isle of Man
Period 4: Creatures of the Night: The Anthropology of Nocturnal Beings
Lunch
Period 5: The Politics of the Supernatural Species
Period 6: Enchanted Engineering

I'd never heard of any of these classes, although some slightly resembled the regular world equivalent.

Taking out a map of the campus, I tried to figure out where my first class was. The school's dizzying layout was giving me a headache.

Leanne read over my shoulder. "I think your first class might be down that hall." Leanne pointed to a hall branching off to the left. "Let's meet outside for lunch."

We broke up and went our separate ways. Even with Leanne's help, I was still late. I stealthily slipped in but forgot to shut the door quietly. The sound of the thick oak door closing reverberated along the stone walls. Thirty heads turned in unison—including the teacher's. My cheeks burned.

"How nice of you to join us," Professor Nightingale commented sarcastically before turning back to the board. "Please take a seat."

I nodded and looked for an empty desk. The students around me whispered to each other, casting nasty glances my way. I took in a shaky breath and began moving down an aisle, spotting a couple of empty chairs towards the back.

I sat down next to a plump girl with fiery red hair, thinking she appeared friendly. But the moment I glanced her way, she looked positively horrified. I smiled, trying to calm her uneasiness, but I no longer had the ability to look innocent. I cringed as she got up and scurried to the next available seat, leaving me to my new status as a social pariah.

I spent the next thirty minutes distracted as Professor Nightingale prattled on about class policies and procedures. Thanks to my heightened hearing, I overheard every mean conversation whispered between classmates, all discussing yours truly. My classmates believed I was a freak, a monster, unnatural, and evil. I tried to stay calm, breathing in and out steadily and silently chanting, “Don’t cry. Don’t cry,” over and over.

I hadn’t been especially liked at my old high school, but at least no one thought I was a monster.

The hateful conversations halted as a voice boomed from above, filling the chamber. “Gabrielle Fiori, please report to the principal’s office.” It took me a minute to realize the message was meant for me; I was busy looking for the nonexistent intercom. I guess they’re useless if you have magic.

Once I realized that I was the student getting publicly humiliated, my gut filled with dread. Apparently this horrible day was going to get worse.

I packed up my notebook, listening to the chorus of whispers, and held my head high as I walked out of room, knowing thirty separate sets of eyes were staring at me.

It was a relief to step into the empty hallway, but now I had to face my own worries. Why was I being called to the principal’s office?

ꙮ ꙮ

Inside the office, Mr. Hazard, Peel’s principal, sat behind a huge desk, intently reading and scribbling on the paper in front of him. I knocked on the opened door, not wanting to startle him.

He looked up, and when he saw me, he rubbed a hand over his face, as though simply thinking of the task at hand made him weary.

"Hello Miss Fiori."

"Um, hi," I said nervously. I walked into his office and tentatively perched on one of the two dark leather seats across from him. I still couldn't possibly fathom why I was in here.

"A young woman came in this morning claiming you threatened her."

Doris. My shame at the previous night's events and the oncoming punishment made me feel feverish.

He continued. "Now normally, as a supernatural academy, we don't deal with these juvenile spats. We understand that it can be difficult for students to deal with their newly Awoken abilities, but we expect all our students to act as mature young adults.

"However, Miss Fiori, threats are taken very seriously. Do you understand?"

I nodded.

"I must impress upon you that your actions could—should—get you expelled."

I held my breath. Was I about to get kicked out of Peel Academy on my first day?

"I'm glad you look concerned." Mr. Hazard eyed my countenance. "It means my decision to let this event slide was not in vain." For the first time since entering his office, he gave a small smile. I let out the breath I was holding.

"But," he stressed, "there are many who are, frankly, disturbed by your presence here. Traditionally, we have never accepted vampires into our school. To put it bluntly, had anyone known this was to happen, Peel would not have sought your attendance.

"However, we cannot undo what has been done, and the academy takes full responsibility for your current state. The best thing that we can do now is to teach you the high morals of the supernatural community."

I was reeling from his words. Peel would not have accepted me had they known? Was being a vampire really *that* bad?

Was I a bad person? I mean, I did scare Doris, and I once bumped a parked car and didn't leave my insurance information.

I shook myself of my doubts. Having a few extra superpowers didn't change who I was.

"How can you say that?" I whispered. "I'm still human."

Principal Hazard looked hard at me. Instead of sympathy, instead of pity, his gaze was flinty. He was one of them. For some unknown reason, he was appalled by my existence. The only surprise was why he hadn't jumped on the opportunity to expel me.

"Human?" he replied. "Only temporarily."

Chapter 11

AFTER MY MEETING with Principal Hazard, I went back to class, but I wasn't mentally present for the rest of the day. Everywhere students whispered about me—in class, in the halls, at lunch. Even fourth period, which should've been bearable because Oliver was in the same class, was soured as soon as I saw Doris's blonde hair and her mean little smile. By the time the final bell rang, I couldn't get out of class fast enough.

My eyes stung as I clumsily jabbed my key a few times into the doorknob. It finally slid through, and I pushed into my room. Thankfully, Leanne hadn't arrived yet. My confident veneer crumbled, and I swiped away a couple rebellious tears.

I remembered some girls hating me in high school,

mistakenly believing I was a threat to their relationships. Now I realized that my siren genes were likely to blame for their boyfriends' wandering eyes and their own insecurities.

But today? Today was different. The hatred directed at me wasn't petty jealousy. It was a deep-rooted fear of things that go bump in the night. Only now, that bump had a face, mine.

I took a couple deep breaths. Wallowing was nice, but only for so long.

My book bag was slumped against the wall, and one of my textbooks peeked out. I pulled it out and looked over the cover. *Living and Dying in a World of Wonder: An Introduction to Supernatural Beings.* It was the book Andre had teased me about a few days ago.

I walked over to my bed and plopped down with the book. I opened it, scanned the table of contents, and flipped to the section on vampires. I passed over the first few sentences about vampires being an abomination and skimmed the rest of the passage.

The true horror of the vampiric condition is not the hapless victims whom the vampire kills, but those whom the vampire saves. This is because the origin of the vampire in the modern era began in 1321, somewhere near Bucharest, Romania.

A Spanish merchant by the name of Salvatore de Leon met and married a Romanian woman during one of his travels.

Near the turn of the fourteenth century they had a child by the name of Andre.

I started at the name. Was I reading Andre's biography? Curious, I read on.

A few years later, the Plague swept through the Romanian village the family lived in at the time, infecting Salvatore's wife. Salvatore prayed to God to save her, but salvation didn't come and his wife died.

Perhaps vampires would not have existed if the Plague had not returned to the tiny Romanian village two decades later. However, that was not to be, and in 1321, Andre, Salvatore's son, was exposed to the illness and slowly began to die.

Salvatore diligently prayed, but when prayer appeared to fail a second time, he cursed God and swore allegiance to the devil in return for the life of his son.

It is said that the next day, a traveling merchant visited the village. The merchant approached Salvatore, saying that he heard Salvatore's cry the night before and could grant his wish upon one condition.

"I will give you what you most desire, the life of your son," the merchant said, "in exchange for what you hold most dear." Salvatore quickly agreed, believing the merchant was asking Salvatore's earthly possessions as payment. But he had no sooner agreed than the merchant showed himself to be the devil, and Salvatore paid with his soul.

Andre, now a man, was wiser than his father. When the devil came for Andre, he told the devil that his immortal soul was safe; Salvatore could not sell any soul other than his own. But the devil was still trickier. "I am not going to take your soul. I am here to heal you, and I will give you something men have sold their souls to possess, for I am benevolent." And he bestowed upon Andre the gift of immortality.

The gift, Andre soon found, was a thinly veiled curse, for he could only feast upon humans and awake at night. He was forbidden from entering hallowed ground. And while he had not forsaken his soul to the devil, the blood on Andre's hands robbed him of forever entering heaven's gates.

And so the curse of vampirism is passed to every new member, for time corrupts even the most innocent.

I stared at the page a few more seconds, disbelieving. I should've been worried about my own immortal soul, but instead I thought about Andre. I couldn't reconcile this Andre, a victim of circumstance, with the Andre I knew—a vain, materialistic, and self-centered individual.

At least I got to the root of everyone's anger. I was destined for evil, and yet, through some loophole, I was allowed to walk the esteemed halls of Peel Academy. It must kill all those self-righteous snobs that the school was responsible for awakening my vampirism.

Out of curiosity I flipped over to the section on sirens. I skimmed over the author's boring commentary, until a section caught my attention.

The siren's power is sexually derived. This can be dangerous if misused, as both men and women can fall completely under their control when this power is exerted. Abuse of power is common, and this is where modern stereotypes of sirens come from.

Less commonly known, these creatures are cursed with misfortune. The writings of Adeodatus follow seven generations of sirens, all of whom were victims of adultery, murder, incest, rape, espionage, treason, or suicide. His records indicate that none of these sirens lived past the age of thirty.

I closed the book and sighed. I really did have some cursed genes.

Leanne and Oliver came in a little while later, only to change and run off to a back-to-school mixer they were invited to.

I tried to not let it get to me that I was obviously not invited. But as I lay on my bed, reading a novel I brought from Los Angeles, I couldn't help but feel antisocial. Back at home I had lots of friends and regularly had plans. Now I was avoided.

Almost as soon as the sun dipped below the horizon, my phone started ringing.

I looked at the caller, not sure who knew my new phone number. I had barely owned the phone a week.

"*Andre?*" I read the caller ID out loud. How was his

number saved onto my phone? Because I didn't add it. And I definitely didn't add the two emoticon hearts next to his name.

I debated whether or not I should answer.

Thinking about the Andre I read about earlier, I clicked "Accept."

"Hello?" I put the phone to my ear.

"I was convinced you weren't going to answer," he said. "How long did you stare at my number before picking up?"

"I thought you were a vampire, not a psychic." How did he know?

I heard the smile in his voice when he responded. "What made you change your mind and pick up?"

"Don't flatter yourself; I was bored. Why are you calling me?"

I could tell he was amused. "I wanted to see how your first day went."

Oh. He was wondering whether I munched on anyone.

He corrected himself. "Actually, I wanted to see how you were. There are a lot of supremacist morons at Peel, and I figured your first day might've been rough."

I cleared my throat. "It was fine," I lied.

"Good. Put on something sexy. Tonight will be your first lesson on being a vampire."

ꙮ ꙮ

Andre drove us up to the front of the club, leaving the idling car for the valets to pick up. Even though it was a Monday, there was still a long line snaking down the street.

The screaming began as fans caught sight of Andre. The sight of so many excited woman—and men—shocked me until I remembered he was an international celebrity.

He waved and smiled, looking cool and collected. The screaming escalated, some women even rushing out of line to get closer. Bodyguards materialized just in time, holding Andre's eager fans back.

Andre came over to where I stood teetering in my uncomfortable heels, and he draped an arm around my waist. I stared at where his hand rested. That was awfully presumptuous of him. I grabbed his hand to peel it away from my waist and cameras went off.

Instead of letting me remove his hand, his fingers curled around my own, and he leaned into me, murmuring, "Just go with it. They want a show."

I bared my teeth at the cameras, trying to fake a grin.

We walked inside, and the thrum of music pounded my ears. Now that we were away from the gawkers, I pushed his hand away, "Just because I came out with you does not mean I'm your date," I yelled over the music.

He gave me a devil-may-care grin. "Fine. Follow me."

We wove in and out of dancers, drunk club goers, and more fans. He led me upstairs. More bodyguards stood by the entrance to what I assumed was the VIP section. Seeing Andre, they opened the doors.

I followed him into a room full of curtained alcoves, where swanky-looking groups of people chatted over their drinks. An entire side of the room was made up of one-way mirrors, so VIP members could look out onto the club without themselves being seen.

He broke away from me and walked over to a table, probably schmoozing with his high-end customers. I walked over to the one-way mirror, and watched as couples danced and friends laughed.

I pushed my wavy hair away from my eyes, and fidgeted with a ring I was wearing. Why was I here? So far I hadn't learned anything remotely vampire-ish, and frankly, this VIP crowd made me uncomfortable.

"We meet again."

I looked up to see Theodore, the Scottish vampire who had laid me out the day before, standing next to me.

"You still owe me an apology." What I had meant to say was *hey*, but even a bad day couldn't completely wipe out my attitude.

"Saucy minx." He laughed and twirled his glass of wine—or some other dark fluid I wasn't willing to dwell on. "No wonder Andre's pursuing you. He so does love the chase."

His words put me in an even fouler mood. "For

your information, Theodore, Andre is *not* pursuing me. He's giving me my first lesson on being a vampire." My explanation sounded weak, even to me, and I briefly considered whether Andre did have an ulterior motive. But I wouldn't let Theodore see any of my personal misgivings. "It's none of your business anyway."

He smiled at me. "That's where you are wrong, tootsie." I gashed my teeth together at his idea of an endearment. "I am Andre's right-hand man. It's my business to know these things. And if Andre's interested in you, it's my job to make sure you are not a threat."

I was shocked.

"Me?" I asked incredulously. "A threat?"

Andre appeared behind us. "Ready?" He looked at me.

"For what?" I asked, momentarily distracted.

"I have more to show you." He turned to Theodore, who was still gazing intensely at me. "Theodore, I'll meet back up with you later tonight."

Theodore nodded and reluctantly left.

"Theodore sucks," I said. "... Pun unintended."

"Theodore is looking out for my best interests," Andre replied. "Now come."

I let Andre lead me through another door. We stepped into a richly decorated private lounge. Crimson velvet couches were placed throughout the room. A series of paintings of Greek gods and goddesses hung along the amber walls. The one-way mirrors here opened onto a balcony.

But the most shocking part was the room's seclusion. We were alone. I couldn't decide whether the presence of psychotic fans and pretentious VIP members was preferable to being alone with Andre.

"I figured you were the type of person who favored small, intimate settings to large crowds," he said.

I tried not to dwell on the way he said *intimate*, which seemed full of sexual undertones. Then again, maybe that was just me.

"Are you pursuing me?" I blurted out, using the same wording Theodore had.

He raised an eyebrow. "*Pursuing*?" He paused long enough to make me feel like an idiot for bringing the subject up altogether. "That would imply that you were prey. And I think we can both agree that's definitely not the case." Why I thought Andre would give me a straight answer was beyond me.

"But," he continued, "when one has lived as long as me, people become predictable—boring. You, however, are anything but."

I looked him in the eye, trying to not be distracted by how beautiful he was. "Sorry to burst your bubble Andre, but I have a soulmate."

"So?"

"So, I'm not going to fall in love with you."

"I wasn't asking for anything nearly so tedious," he said. "Perhaps we could start with friendship?"

I snorted. Fat chance we were going to be friends. But I'd play nice.

"Fine."

The sounds of the club dully thrummed through the room, and the song that came on caught my attention. The melody coursed through me.

I walked over to the doors that led to the balcony, transfixed by the music. Andre came over, unlatched the door for me, and followed me out.

"What song is this?" I asked, completely overtaken by the melody.

He was silent for so long I figured he hadn't heard me over the music.

"You've never heard it, I can promise you that. It's forbidden from distribution in most countries."

Go figure.

"Why is it forbidden?" I asked, distracted.

He gazed at the crowd, who were completely lost in the music. Seeing all their empty eyes sobered me up.

"This song was sung by a siren—by your mother in fact."

My head whipped around, the song's spell broken. "This is my mother singing?" So much for not appearing too eager where my past was concerned.

He nodded.

"Did you know her?"

He nodded, a few loose strands of his hair falling forward as he leaned on the ledge. "Yes, I knew her."

I wanted to flood him with questions, but the

strange sound of my mother's voice kept distracting me. "What's wrong with her voice?"

"She is using glamour. It's one of your powers as well. It's the ability to bespell others."

This was the second time I'd heard about this power, but I was skeptical that I actually had this ability. Wouldn't I have already felt it?

"Luckily the glamour is diluted by the recording, and anyway, Celeste is only singing about enjoying the moment. Pretty harmless. But still, it's outlawed in most places because the song bespells listeners without their explicit consent."

I listened to the lyrics.

Carpe diem they say,
Seize the day,
Because before long,
Tomorrow will dawn,
And you will be gone.

"I read about sirens. You were right. Apparently we don't last long."

"I know." He was solemn. "Lucky for you, your vampire genes gave you a back up plan."

I gave him a long look. "I read about vampires too. And it seems like a pretty lousy back up plan if you ask me."

In the background, my mother was still singing. I got chills hearing her voice. She might be dead, but not forgotten.

Andre's phone rang. He pulled it out and looked at the number. "I need to take this. I'll be just a moment. When I get back we'll begin." And like that, I was alone.

I walked out onto the balcony. Leaning over the ledge, I raptly listened to the rest of the song. Once it was over, I watched the crowd slowly awaken from the song. They were invigorated.

I went back inside, feeling like I was an interloper on their fun.

When I tried closing the door behind me, it wouldn't latch. I jiggled it, and tried to force the lock into place. Distracted, I mistook the light tread of footfalls behind me for Andre.

Until someone grabbed a fistful of my hair.

Yanking my head back, my attacker placed a sharp knife at my throat.

In a gravelly voice, the man spoke in my ear. "If you move an inch, I will slit your throat."

Chapter 12

I RAISED MY hands in surrender, barely breathing. How did an attacker get inside the most guarded room in the club?

"Good. Now follow my instructions exactly. I am going to calmly lead you out of here as though nothing's wrong. If you scream or otherwise alert anyone that that's not the case, I will kill you—don't think I won't either. I promise you, I mean every word." He said this with such lethal coolness that I believed him.

But I'd also watched enough CourtTV to know that once I left the premise with him, my chances of survival drastically decreased. And that realization was the straw that broke the camel's back. I'd had a really shitty day already, and I. Just. Couldn't. Take it. Anymore.

From within me I felt something release, and a wave of power washed over me.

Moving fast, I grabbed the hand that held the knife to my throat and squeezed. He screamed and dropped the knife.

Using the arm I held as leverage, I catapulted him over my shoulder, vaguely impressed I could throw a grown man across the room. He hit the far wall and slid down.

I walked over to where he lay gasping, put a hand to his throat, and squeezed. "What do you want with me?"

"Abomination," he wheezed. And then he threw me off of him.

I skidded along the floor, but before I had the chance to get up, he was on top of me. He cocked an arm back and punched me repeatedly in the face. Something crunched, and blood poured from my nose. The smell of it triggered something primal, and I felt my canines elongate in response. My nose stung badly, and my eyes teared up from the pain.

Believing me sufficiently incapacitated, he stood up and picked up the knife where he dropped it. I backed up, still on my back. My self-defense classes hadn't prepared me for this. I didn't know how to fight, and this guy did. But I had more to lose.

Almost casually the man walked back over to me. He kneeled down over my body. "Hmm, if you won't leave quietly, I'll just have to kill you now." He ran a hand down my face, toying with me. My attacker was enjoying this. Enjoying my pain and the slow process of ending another life.

I moved quickly, kicking him swiftly in the chest. He fell back, and I followed him. We rolled together, grappling for possession of the knife. I grabbed his free hand and bent his wrist back until I heard a snap. He howled in agony, and I made the mistake of relaxing. With his good hand he sliced the dagger down my cheek and drove it towards my heart. I jerked my body to the side at the last minute, and my attacker plunged the knife into my shoulder. I screamed.

Behind us the door opened, and then a roar eclipsed my scream. I saw the whites of my attacker's eyes a second before his body was torn away from mine and flung across the room like a rag doll. I heard the sickening crack as his body hit the far wall and the plaster gave.

Andre stood at my feet, looking like a fallen angel. A very pissed off fallen angel.

"Take him away!" I heard him order his bodyguards.

Andre bent over me, concerned. "I am so sorry," he whispered.

Andre's gaze flicked to the knife that was still plunged in my shoulder before shifting back to me.

"I need you to stare me in the eyes," he commanded. "Don't look away."

I glanced at his hand, which he'd wrapped around

the hilt of the dagger.

"No," I whimpered.

"Gabrielle, focus on me. Focus." I stared into his eyes and felt everything fall away. It was just him, me, and that whimsical feeling I could really get used to. And then it all shattered as Andre yanked the knife out of my shoulder.

The scream ripped from me.

"Shhhh." Andre soothed me like I was a small child. Someone handed him a towel, and he used it to halt the bleeding. It took many minutes for the pain and nausea to become manageable.

"Aren't you supposed to give me a drink before you go about pulling out knives?"

That earned a chuckle. "I can't be giving alcohol to minors. I might lose my liquor license."

I rolled my eyes. As if Andre actually followed the rules.

"I think my nose is broken," I said.

He glanced down at my nose. "Then it already healed itself."

"*What?*" I realized the pain in my face *had* lessened. "How is that possible?"

He picked me up, somehow managing to shrug even as he carried me.

"Vampires heal much more rapidly than normal humans," he said.

We passed back into the VIP common room, where people huddled in clusters, some with their camera phones pulled out, taking shots of us.

"I can walk, really," I said, struggling against him. Reluctantly he put me down. "So vampires heal quickly. But I'm still human, aren't I?"

A crease appeared right between Andre's eyebrows. I tried not to think about how breathtakingly gorgeous he looked.

"Gabrielle, I think we can agree that you haven't been completely human since you woke up in the hospital. Your nose is proof that your body already has the ability to return itself to its original state. This same ability keeps vampires frozen at whatever age they were changed."

"So what does that mean?" I asked.

He only shook his head. "I don't know."

ꟷ ꟷ

When we approached the onsite paramedics, there was not much left for them to mend. The bruising on my face had lightened to a nasty yellow color—apparently this was a good thing—and the knife wound on my face had almost completely healed.

Most surprising of all, my shoulder wound had closed up, making stiches unnecessary.

The next few hours were weary. I repeated my story over and over to the police. Luckily the police—and just about everyone else on the island—happened to be supernaturals, which made telling the truth a whole lot easier. My assailant was in custody, and the police force was currently running a background check.

Eventually, Andre rescued me. For once I appreciated his pushy ways. He pulled some strings and got me out of the police station before 1:00 a.m.

I met him at the entrance, where he was sitting in one of the vinyl chairs. I laughed. I couldn't help it. The sight of him dwarfing the seat in the sitting room of the police station, clad in his designer clothes, was ridiculous.

"Inspector O'Reilly wanted me to give you her *best* regards," I said, walking towards him.

At some point today, my opinion of Andre had drastically changed. Maybe it was that he reached out to me when I had been feeling like a social pariah, or maybe it was his tragic history. Or maybe it was that he saved my life.

He gave me a smoldering look, one eyebrow arching up.

"Oh, cut the brooding crap," I said, walking past him to push the door open, "Thanks for getting me out of there."

Andre followed me out. "So that's it?" he asked. "You're going to act as though you didn't nearly die two hours ago?"

I stopped in my tracks and faced him, the chilly night air prickling my skin. "How am I supposed to act?"

"Bothered. Scared."

"I am bothered, and I am scared. Happy?"

"No."

I looked at him curiously. "Why do you care?"

"It's my job to protect you." He looked angry.

I closed my eyes. "Just because I am your newest member does not mean you're entitled to question why I act the way I act."

"I am when you are blatantly cavalier about your life!" He ran a ticked-off hand through his hair. "Being what you are, the price is much too high."

"My soul is fine. I already know it's time that screws all you vampires over."

He quieted down. "I wasn't talking about that."

I was surprised. "Then what were you talking about?"

He opened his mouth to speak, thought better, and shook his head. "Never mind. Let's get you back. We'll reschedule training."

We got into the car, and Andre pulled out of the police station.

I ran my fingers over the upholstery, thinking about the fears I buried deep. "Who was he?" My voice was so quiet I wasn't sure I spoke the words at all. "The man who tried to kill me?"

Andre's hands tightened on the steering wheel. "Scum." He looked over at me. "The police didn't tell you who your attacker was?"

I watched the scenery fly by as Andre accelerated down the dark city streets. "All they told me was that he was currently in custody, and they were doing a background check." I was glad Andre had turned the guy in. I got the distinct impression that most people who crossed Andre disappeared. I couldn't say why, but I was relieved my attacker hadn't died.

Andre muttered something about incompetent police, but to me he said, "Your attacker is Timothy Watts, a laid-off construction worker and an alcoholic. More importantly, he is one hundred percent human."

"What?" I shook my head. "That's not possible. The man threw me across the room, and he moved quicker than I've ever seen a human move." I remembered my own inhuman feat of strength. I had also tossed a person—a full-grown man—across the room. Then I remembered what other physiological changes my powers brought on.

"Damn," I said.

Andre looked over as I felt my canines. They seemed normal.

"Ah," he said, recognizing what I was doing. "Did your fangs come out earlier?"

"Yeah. It was the smell of my blood."

He nodded. "Blood, pheromones, and adrenaline will trigger it."

"*Pheromones?*"

He shrugged. "Pheromones can be a powerful aphrodisiac for a vampire."

I cringed. *Ew.*

He laughed at my expression. "You're not going to be so grossed out when it happens." His laughter was distracting, full and rich.

"Anyway," I said, getting back onto our previous topic. "Why was this Timothy guy trying to kill me?"

"I don't know. The police think he was going to kidnap you for ransom money."

I shook my head. "That doesn't make any sense. First off, I have no money. But second, and more important, the guy was going to kill me. I'm absolutely certain about that."

Andre growled, sending shivers up my arms. "What doesn't make any sense is how he got into my VIP suite in the first place—and why he would attack you in such a highly protected location. That room should be impenetrable."

I gazed out the window at the nightlife beyond the road. The most amazing thing about my new vision was how alive the world was at night.

Andre's phone chirped.

Smoothly he pulled it out of his pocket and to his ear. "Andre."

I could hear the other end of the conversation, and, unashamed, I proceeded to eavesdrop. "This is Sergeant O'Brien."

I tried not to roll my eyes as I waited for her to flirt with Andre. Instead, she said, "Timothy Watts just escaped custody and is at large."

Chapter 13

ANDRE SWORE. "WHY wasn't anyone paying attention to him? I paid good money for your department to make this a priority case."

Now *that* was news to me.

"Sir, we have no idea how he could have escaped. The officer watching him says the man vanished right into thin air." If I wasn't mistaken, Officer O'Brien was a little shaken.

Andre's lips thinned in displeasure. "Margaret," he said, "*humans* don't just disappear into thin air. Find him."

Officer O'Brien sounded weary. "We will notify you of any and all updates. Have a good night."

Andre clicked off the phone and pounded a fist

into the driving wheel, denting it as he did so.

His jaw muscle twitched. "You heard everything she said?" he asked.

"You mean the part about Timothy Watts escaping? Yep, heard that." My hands had begun to shake. Was Timothy Watts going to come after me again? Would I have to live in fear of another attack?

"This day just needs to be over," I mumbled.

"You should stay with me at the mansion," he said.

I raised my eyebrows. "I don't think so."

He looked up at the car's ceiling—really unsafe when considering how fast he was going. "We have guest rooms Gabrielle."

"Well, I want to sleep in my own bed. My building has decent security." A.k.a., a college student at the front desk.

"Fine." Andre wasn't buying it, but for once he didn't argue. Instead he said, "I meant to tell you this much earlier this evening, but got sidetracked: Santiago left you an inheritance, and I scheduled a meeting for you with the manager of his estate later this week."

My heart skipped a beat. My biological father wrote me into his will? Why had I not known about this? "How do you know that my father left me an inheritance?"

"All vampires write out wills, and Santiago left me in charge of carrying out his. I actually hadn't thought about the matter until yesterday. I looked into it, and it appears that Santiago's assets have remained frozen since his death."

I wasn't sure how to respond to this news. My father had become a shadowy figure in my memory. I was so young when he died that almost everything about him—even his name—had all but been forgotten. All that I knew for certain was that I loved him and that he saved me from that fire.

"Santiago left behind peculiar instructions. Instructions that his inheritance go to you, and further that, in the case of your disappearance, the inheritance was to be frozen for up to twenty years. All that he owns is yours—and believe me, it's a lot."

ꕥ ꕥ

I woke up to a pillow smacking me in the face.

"You're a loser." Leanne sat on my bed, arms crossed. She was still in her pajamas and her hair was a mess. "You were almost murdered last night, and you didn't bother waking me up!"

I rubbed my eyes. Behind Leanne, I read the letters brightly illuminated on her laptop:

ATTEMPTED MURDERER AT LARGE.
INVESTIGATORS CLAIM PERPETRATOR VANISHED INTO THIN AIR.

I yawned. "Right. Because I want to relive my attack at 2:00 a.m. in the morning—when we have class the next day."

She paused. "I guess that's a good point." I could tell Leanne was still agitated, and it took me a second to realize that it wasn't me she was angry with.

Understanding dawned on me. "Are you upset because you didn't see it happen?"

"*Foresee*—seers foresee," she corrected absentmindedly. "And yes, I should've been able to foresee this like I did the fight with Doris." She frowned.

"Leanne, don't be so hard on yourself. You just developed the ability a few days ago."

"Yeah," she agreed halfheartedly. Her voice indicated that she was going to still blame herself.

There was a bang as someone tried to open our locked door. Leanne and I grabbed each other.

"Bitches, let me in!"

Oliver. I let out a shaky breath, got up, and unlocked the door. He pushed his way in before enveloping me in a hug. "Stop almost dying on me beautiful."

When he pulled away, I saw his eyes were red rimmed.

"Aw, Oliver," I hugged him back, "I'm pretty tough to kill."

He wiped his eyes, composing himself. He took in the two of us and made a tsk-ing sound. "Whoa. You two put the *hag* in *haggard*."

That earned him a pillow to the face.

ꙮ ꙮ

Today was going a lot like yesterday. Everyone acted as though I was the bubonic plague. By the time I walked into my third period class, History of the Isle of Man, I had adjusted to the disgust and fear I saw in most students' eyes. When would they realize I was just like them?

I made my way down a row of desks. Predictably, those closest to me scooted their desks away—as if my mere proximity would somehow affect them.

I managed to find a series of empty desks near the back of the room, and I picked one and sat down.

I was left to my dark thoughts until a sexy guy with wavy blonde hair entered the room. The girls noticed him instantly. They followed him with their eyes as he made his way through the class. I could hear the subtle increase of the room's collective heart rate, and I could even smell the adrenaline of a few girls who had some serious crushes.

He passed them, making a beeline for ... me. I stared into a pair of baby blues as he sat down next to me, looking like a golden god.

"Hey," he said casually, his voice thick with an Australian accent. He leaned back in his chair and stretched, oblivious to the attention he was receiving.

"Uh, hi," I replied, surprised someone wanted to talk to me.

"I'm Caleb Jennings."

I looked around us, sure this had to be a mistake or some sort of prank. "I'm Gabrielle," I said.

The bell rang, and our teacher approached the front of the class.

"Did I miss anything yesterday?" Caleb asked. "I was out."

I whispered back. "Only a series of Manx terms for different geographical regions. Absolutely riveting."

Caleb stared at me for a moment, and then broke out into laughter.

Mr. Mead gave us the stink eye, but he didn't stop talking to scold us.

"I heard Mr. Mead is supposed to be epically boring," Caleb said.

"Really—you heard that? Your source must've confused our teacher with someone else. Like I said, this guy's absolutely riveting." Caleb snickered.

Two girls turned to give me dirty looks. They turned back around and leaned into each other. I could hear their whispered accusation: *Why is* he *sitting with* her? *And why is he talking to her?* I was wondering the same thing myself.

As the class got going, and the professor discussed the history of the Isle of Man, Caleb passed a paper to me.

I looked over at him, and he smiled before continuing to take notes. I opened the note to find a game of hangman. The sentence that I was to figure out, letter by letter, ended with a question mark. As we passed the note back and forth, and I was seriously losing, the hanged man began looking an awful lot like Professor

Mead with his monocle and neatly trimmed beard.

Eventually I decoded the message.

Will you go out with me Friday night?

I quickly looked over at Caleb, who was waiting for my answer.

Going on a date would be a lost cause. For one, my past experiences had never ended well. The only person to ever pursue me further than a single date was Andre, and well, I didn't really know what to think of that situation.

Two, I was a soulmate. The odds were next to impossible that Caleb was my single true love.

Even knowing it would end badly, I wrote *yes* below his hangman game along with my number.

He smiled brightly and began humming as he went back to his notes, while I sat there trying to tune back in to the lecture and already regretting my decision.

"... The *Mauthe Doog*, or *Moddey Dhoo*, is a black demonic dog that is said to roam these very halls.

"It is believed to be a death knell; anyone who sees the dog will supposedly die soon after." The bell rang, interrupting today's oh-so-exciting discussion of demonic dogs.

"Remember to study your Manx names and read the first chapter of the *History and Myths of the Isle of Man* for Friday's quiz. Class dismissed."

While I was still packing, Caleb grabbed his bag

and slung it over his shoulder. "See you tomorrow," he said, and then he was gone.

ꕥ ꕥ

After school I wandered into the library. Now that my genetics were at the center of a controversy, I needed information about my parents. I didn't know if I'd find anything, but I figured the supernatural community was fairly small. Hopefully that made it more likely that someone had recorded my parents' lives.

The library was barren except for what appeared to be a witch reading up on her spells.

Reading through the catalogue signs, I came to an aisle marked *Monsters*.

I walked down the isle, reading the subcategories. Aquatic Beasts. Otherworld Creatures. Nocturnal Beings.

Bingo.

My eyes skimmed over books on demons, doppelgangers, and lycanthropes before finally finding books on vampires. I pulled out a few books that looked good and headed to a table.

Clicking on the desk lamp, I opened the first book, *Famous Vampires of History*. Sitting right in the middle of the table of contents was my father's name, Santiago Fiori. I knew that he and I shared last names, so I wasn't sure why it was so shocking to see it written on the page. Maybe it was because I hadn't expected to find him so easily after so many years of dead ends. Or maybe it was because the book was first printed in 1887. I flipped to the corresponding chapter.

Born in Venice in 1498, Santiago Fiori was the youngest of the Five Elders and the last vampire sired by Andre de Leon.

Andre had changed my father?

Raptly I read through the next ten pages, finding out that Santiago befriended a number of popes—which shocked and greatly embarrassed the supernatural community—helped smuggle out many aristocratic families during the French Revolution, and had rubbed elbows with Shakespeare—who he later admitted was a "charming brute." And there was so much more. He was a bitter enemy of Henry VIII, a confidante of Napoleon, and a close friend to Benjamin Franklin during the time the latter spent in Europe. It appeared my father went wherever history went.

There was likely to be more information about my father's life throughout the twentieth century, but the book was old, and its history stopped a century short.

I picked up another book, *Modern Day Vampires.* Just like in the previous book, this one discussed my father. While it touched on some of his historical achievements, it focused more on his personality and what he was doing up until the time of his death.

Fiori was an avid supporter of Andre de Leon's Vida Mandata, the official declaration that prohibits vampires from turning a human. He was the only Elder to not pass on his vampiric lineage.

Toward the end of his life, Santiago met, fell in love with, and married Celeste Kallos, the last living siren.

Celeste Kallos. I had found my mother's name. I shut the book. Now it was time to learn about my mother. I got up and wandered the isles, eventually coming across a promising section.

"You're not going to find her here."

I looked up from where I was crouching and met the gaze of an old woman with skin the color of ebony, Peel's head librarian. I read her nametag: Lydia Thyme.

"I'm sorry?" I asked, confused by her words.

"Your mama. You won't find the truth about her in these books. They don't talk about the darker side of your world. For that you need permission to access your clan's private collection."

"How did you know that ... ?" The woman raised an eyebrow and swept her gaze across the library. She didn't need to speak; her eyes said it all. She could read me like the many books around us.

"I'm sorry—I'm still getting used to this new world."

"That's alright, hun. Like I said, if you want to find out more about Celeste, you'll need permission to access your clan's books."

"How do I get access if I'm the last of my clan?"

"In that case I'm afraid students are only allowed in if they are interning with the House of Keys or training with the Politia."

I'd only understood about half of the words in that sentence, but enough to know I didn't have access.

"However, I think under the circumstances surrounding your past and your lineage, I can bend the rules."

"Thank you," I whispered. I'd been met with so much animosity lately that I greatly valued her offer.

"If you can wait here, I'll grab the book I believe you're looking for."

"Yes, definitely."

She inclined her head, and walked down the isle and out of sight. Five minutes later she returned with a single book. She passed it to me, and I read the cover. *The Last of the Sirens*.

"That book should answer all your questions. Make sure you bring the book back to me before you leave."

"Why are you doing this?"

She stared at me for a long time, and I got the distinct impression she was looking into my soul. Finally she said, "I was leading the ritual the night you died. You ... *intrigued* me. I also happen to be old friends with someone from your past."

The hairs on my arm rose. She was trying to tell me something, but I was not sure what. I was also not sure how I should feel about her. She didn't seem evil, like the man in the suit, but she didn't seem good either.

ꟿ ꟿ

I walked back to the table and opened this final book. A bookmark slid out. Never taking my eyes off the text, I fruitlessly groped around for the fallen slip of paper.

My eye caught the title of the final chapter, "The Last of the Sirens." Bookmark forgotten, I flipped to the end of the book.

I skimmed through the history of the Kallos lineage for a few pages before I found what I was looking for.

Celeste Kallos was the last siren to make it to adulthood.

I skimmed through her childhood, which was interesting, but not currently important, until I found a section of text that seemed relevant.

After a successful entrance into the music industry, Celeste began living with Santiago Fiori, a union considered quite controversial by the supernatural world.

Four years later, Celeste gave birth to Santiago's daughter, Gabrielle Fiori. Some found the news miraculous, others a sign of the apocalypse, and others still debunked the idea, claiming the child was the result of an outside relationship. The couple refused to do a paternity test, knowing that the outcome would expose them to negative media attention.

But the test didn't make a difference. On a bright spring morning, police found the body of Celeste abandoned on the side of an English country road. Evidence led investigators to believe it was a hate crime.

I closed the book. I didn't need to read the rest. I wiped away a stray tear. I'd found the answers I was looking for. A father who was sired by Andre de Leon and killed by fire. A mother who was born into a dying race and murdered by hate. This was my legacy.

ꟿ ꟿ

When I entered my dorm room that evening, Leanne was lacing up a pair of hiking shoes. Next to her sat an open satchel filled with empty Ziploc bags.

"Going somewhere?" I asked, eyebrows raised.

"I have some clan homework. Want to come with?"

"Where exactly are you going?"

"There's a shady grove near an entrance to the Otherworld. The herbs that grow there are especially powerful for divining the future."

"Sounds safe."

Leanne rolled her eyes. "Says the girl who plays with vampires and dodges hit men."

"Touché."

"So, are you coming?"

I sighed. "Count me in."

I had just changed into something outdoorsy when

Oliver barged into our room. “Hey ladies—” He took in our outfits. “Where are you guys going, and why wasn’t I invited?”

“We’ll be out in the wilderness, and hiking is involved,” Leanne said as she threw a couple empty vials into her bag. “I assumed it went without saying.”

Oliver put his hands on his hips and turned to me. “It does *not* go without saying.”

I looked at him incredulously. “You actually want to come along?”

He sniffed. “I happened to love the outdoors. I am a fairy after all.”

ᘓ ᘐ

“I hate you both,” Oliver said as the branch I let go of wacked him in the face. “Why did you make me come along?”

“I thought you *loved* the outdoors,” I said, snickering. Oliver muttered something not so nice under his breath.

“Aren’t we near your home?”

“Trust me, the Otherworld leaves plenty to be desired. I’d choose this world any day,” he said.

“Fair enough.”

Suddenly Leanne dropped to her knees. I thought she had found what she was looking for until she lurched forward. Before she hit her head, I managed to catch her. Not realizing that we had stopped, Oliver tripped over the two of us and pitched forward.

"Aiiieeeee!" he squealed. I heard a splat and then, "Ugh, mud! My designer jeans are ruined!"

I ignored Oliver and held Leanne as her eyes stared beyond me, watching something only she could see. After thirty seconds she was back.

She blinked a few times. "Sorry about that. There's powerful magic out here."

"What did you see?" I asked.

Her brows furrowed. "I'm not sure. It all happened in the dark. But it looked like two men—they were definitely criminals. All I really caught was that they were listening to a soccer game on the radio—so they must've been in a car. I think someone else was there, but I can't be sure. It was so dark."

"Do all your premonitions happen this way?"

"Pretty much," Leanne sat up, "although they are usually less forceful than that one."

Oliver moaned a few feet away. "Oh, I see how it is. No one cares about me. Please, continue chatting about visions."

"We better go help the princess," Leanne said.

We got Oliver back on his feet and began walking again—albeit to the chorus of his complaints. Ahead of us the forest brightened, hurting my eyes.

"I think we're almost there," I said, mesmerized by the ethereal beauty of what I was seeing. This must be the grove.

The wind carried a melody, sung by some unseen

being. I wondered how Oliver and Leanne were experiencing this. For me it was easy to imagine a nearby door to the Otherworld.

Before we got closer, Leanne said, "I think we should stop here. We don't want to accidently annoy the wee folk."

"Too late," Oliver chimed in, "you already have."

"You should've just stayed home like I said."

"Hmph."

We spent the better part of an hour groping for herbs. My night vision hardly helped, since I had no idea how to distinguish plants.

It was as I leaned against a tree, taking a break, that I heard a chuckle. I whipped around.

The man in the suit. The wee folk. An attacker. The thoughts quickly entered and exited my mind as Andre stepped out of the shadows.

The pulse of energy that usually accompanied him was absent, probably tampered down by the stronger thrum of the Otherworld. I breathed him in; the scent of expensive cologne barely covered up a masculine smell that was distinctly Andre.

"Cute outfit," he said, running his eyes over my tennis shoes, tight exercise pants, and fitted shirt—and probably a few leaves that clung to them.

"What are you doing here? And how did you find me?" I hissed, alarmed by his presence and annoyed that he was laughing at me.

He smirked, his eyes roving over me. "I have my

ways." He turned his attention to Oliver, who was sitting up in a tree to avoid the mud, and Leanne, who crouched behind a cluster of shrubs, before looking back at me.

"Playing hide-and-go-seek with your friends?" I narrowed my eyes. "You should've asked me. I play a much more fun version."

I rubbed my temples. "Please, Andre not now ..."

His smile faded and he got serious. "You should be more careful. Being out here with these two might actually be more unsafe than being out at night alone."

He comes from a different time. Don't freak out. Don't freak out.

He folded his arms, waiting for my reaction.

"Why exactly, are you here?" I managed to say.

"Escorting you to claim your father's inheritance—unless of course you don't want the small fortune he left for you."

ഇ ഉ

My "small" fortune ended up being over three hundred million dollars. I choked on my coffee, which Andre had bought for me after we'd left my friends at the dorms.

"Congratulations Ms. Fiori, you are now a millionaire—a few times over," said Mr. Taylor, the manager of my father's estate. I smoothed down my shirt to do something with my hands. Thankfully I'd showered and changed before I came.

According to Andre, Mr. Taylor was another seer—a type of supernatural I was beginning to suspect was quite common—and his talents allowed him to successfully manage the accounts of several high-profile supernaturals, including my dad.

Three hundred million dollars. That was more money than I'd ever dreamed of owning. While Andre waited in the lobby, Mr. Taylor and I went over how the money was to be distributed to me, suggestions for investing the money, and a referral to another man who I should talk to.

I thanked him for his help. As I got up to go, he said, "Oh, and one more thing Ms. Fiori."

I paused. His tone had changed. "Your father left something for you in a safety deposit box with instructions that, if you ever found me and claimed your inheritance, you should access it as soon as possible."

If I ever claimed my inheritance? Was my father hoping or expecting that I wouldn't?

"He left the box number and the key with me." Mr. Taylor handed me an envelope that contained the key and the instructions for accessing the deposit box.

His hand shook slightly as I took the envelope from him. Spooked by his reaction, I asked, "What's in it?"

He rubbed his thick salt and pepper mustache. "I don't know, but whatever it is, it was of utmost importance to him that you receive it."

He turned away from me, busying himself by putting away his pen and notepad.

Then I smelled it—fear. I knew Mr. Taylor wasn't scared of me. We'd been talking for over an hour, so I would've picked up on his fear by now if I were the cause. No, this was something much, much worse than an undead teenager.

I leaned over the desk. "What are you not telling me?"

Reluctantly he refocused on me. I could see the whites of his eyes. "Whatever is in that safety deposit box indirectly killed a five-hundred-year-old vampire. Be careful of whom you trust. Sometimes knowledge from the dead has a way of cursing the living."

Chapter 14

THE TWINKLING LIGHTS and softly lit lamps cast a warm glow throughout the French restaurant. Off in the distance I could hear the ocean crashing on the shore. Andre watched me from across the table, looking so handsome it hurt.

"You ready?"

I paused, my soupspoon poised in the air, midway to my mouth. "Ready for what?" After we had left Mr. Taylor's office, Andre had insisted on taking me out to dinner. Considering it was 9:00 p.m., and I hadn't eaten since lunch, I took him up on his offer.

"This is where our first lesson will begin." Of course inviting me to dinner came with strings attached.

I put my soupspoon down, and looked around the

room. Couples quietly chatted over their meals. It was the epitome of civility.

"Here?" I could understand Andre taking me to a club, where people were boiled down to their most primal natures. And I could understand Andre taking me to the middle of nowhere to practice, where I wouldn't be a threat. But here? It was a bit underwhelming.

"Yes. First I want you to practice reading people by their pheromones." His eyes briefly scanned the room before landing on a young couple. "Start with them, and tell me what their scents tell you."

"Uh ... you want me to smell them?" I asked. "Should I get up and go over to them?"

"See first if you can smell anything from here."

Andre had officially lost it. Not only was the room filled with the overpowering smell of food, people had perfume and cologne on.

The thought triggered a memory. When I met up with Andre a few hours earlier, I could smell his scent underneath the cologne. Maybe it would work after all.

Slowly I breathed in the smells of the restaurant. I began tracing the much more overpowering smells back to their origins, getting the hang of it. I quickly sorted out the overpowering smells of food and perfume, and focused on the fainter but more primal smells. It was like distinguishing colors.

I followed the different scents back to their various

owners until I caught the young woman's. She was smiling, but a familiar cloying scent betrayed her.

I turned to Andre. "She's scared."

Andre only smiled. "Now the man."

It took me a few minutes to sort out which smell led back to him. When I did, I couldn't place the scent. I looked at Andre, but he gave me nothing, so I guessed. "Guilt?"

"Can you confirm it?"

"How could I possibly—" And then I smelled it. It was the smell of another woman, and it was all over his skin. "Ugh, gross! I think I'm going to be sick." The man was cheating on his girlfriend, and he had the audacity to not even take a shower before meeting up with her.

Andre raised an eyebrow.

"Yes, it's definitely guilt."

"Good. You did fantastic. One of the benefits and frustrations of being a vampire is being able to sort out smells. It's a great tool for reading people, and eventually it will be how you figure out who is willing to let you take their blood."

"Ew." I hugged myself, no longer hungry.

He ignored my response—as usual. "Smell can also be a huge distraction, both because when you're in a crowded setting, it's hard to distinguish separate smells, and because there are those who purposefully manipulate vampires with smell. Considering you were almost killed the other day because you didn't sense your attacker, it is especially vital for you to know the boundaries of your abilities."

My hackles rose at his last comment. "You expected me to *sense* my attacker in that sexpot club of yours? While my dead mother was bespelling the clubbers?" My voice rose at the end of the sentence, and a few of the nearby couples glanced over at us.

Andre's eyes thinned. "Of course not. You are ignorant when it comes to our world. But that is my point—"

"If you're going to call me ignorant, then I'm leaving."

"Until you learn, Gabrielle, you *are* ignorant."

I stood up and threw down my napkin. "I think I'm done for the evening."

Andre stood up as well, and his height was staggering and oppressive. "We're not finished yet."

"Oh yes we are." I pushed past him and walked out of the restaurant.

He followed behind me. "Gabrielle." He spoke calmly, yet there was a distinct sense of authority to his voice. "This is not optional, and you cannot—and will not—disobey me."

His statement pissed me off. I turned and yelled at him. "This is not the 1300s, I am not your slave, and you cannot command me—you giant misogynist!"

His hands clenched. "I am your king!" His voice boomed.

I turned away from him—big mistake.

He whipped me back to face him. Only his eyes were no longer filled with anger. Desire flashed in them a second before our lips met.

The energy that always thrummed when he was near became a living, breathing thing. It danced from my skin to his and back again.

My surprise faded into passion, and I responded to his kiss. I heard him groan, and the kiss deepened. He gathered me up and held me like a drowning man holding onto a life raft. I wrapped my arms around his neck, consumed by the kiss as our energy circuited through us.

Eventually—reluctantly—we split apart.

"Gabrielle ..." he said, his voice low and his eyes deep. "I think—"

Laughter interrupted his words. The hair along my flesh rose. He was here, the man in the suit.

"Oh God ..." I backed away from Andre.

"Gabrielle, what's wrong?" Concern had crept into his voice.

"You mean you didn't hear it?"

"Hear what?" He was looking at me curiously.

"Laughter."

Then I saw him, beyond Andre's shoulder. He was hardly more than a darker shadow amongst the shadows. I put a hand to my mouth.

Andre turned quickly and followed my gaze, scanning the area. But even though the man in the suit made no effort to hide, Andre couldn't see him. I already knew that no humans could see him, but I had desperately hoped that supernaturals could.

"Let's get you home." He led me back to his car.

We buckled up and pulled out of the parking lot. I glanced behind me and watched the man in the suit walk out of the shadows and stand underneath the artificial light of a nearby lamppost.

You can't ever hide. His voice tickled the flesh around my ear and I flinched.

Andre looked over. A crease had formed between his brows. "What's going on?"

"What do you mean?" I knew what he meant, but I was not going to give up information easily.

"You're frightened. I can smell it all over you."

I should've known; we'd just been going over smells. "I thought I saw someone."

"Who?"

I wasn't sure how to respond. The man in the suit had always been my little secret. While I knew I wasn't crazy, I also knew that sane people just didn't see apparitions.

I decided to go for honesty. "I don't know."

He raised an eyebrow and looked over at me. "You mean to tell me that you saw someone you don't know, and you are scared of them?"

"It's more complicated than that."

"I bet. Because right now I don't believe you."

I leaned my forehead on my hand. He was reaffirming what I already knew; no one would believe me.

Andre pulled the car over. Nothing but rolling hills and farmland surrounded us. The car idled as he faced me. "You know you can trust me, right? I will never vilify you, and I will never think you're crazy. Whatever has you worked up is not a burden you have to carry on your own." His eyes had gone soft again, and he reached over to comfort me.

His words and gaze made my stomach flutter in a way that all his beauty couldn't. What I felt wasn't lust ... it was something far scarier. Something I wasn't ready to admit to.

Gently I moved his hand away. "You can't understand. But more than that, this is not your problem, and you cannot protect me from my own troubles."

ꕥ ꕥ

The next few days passed uneventfully. Which, for the moment, was a really good thing. I used the time to catch up on my reading assignments. Unfortunately, this also gave me time to think over my close brush with death, my inheritance, and—most distracting—my kiss with Andre.

Friday morning, Leanne got ready next to me, leaning in front of her mirror and putting on mascara.

"So," she said, "there's supposed to be a college party tonight off campus. You up for going with me and Oliver? It's a themed party."

I fidgeted; I still hadn't told her about my plans

with Caleb. "Actually," I said with faked nonchalance, "I have a date tonight."

"No way!" she exclaimed, turning to look at me. "Why didn't you say anything? Wait—who are you going on a date with?"

"Caleb Jennings," I said, uncomfortable. "I met him in one of my classes." I hadn't mentioned it before because Caleb had been absent for most of the week. To be honest, I wasn't even sure we were still going out tonight until he sent me a series of texts confirming our date was still on.

"Oh, he's a hottie for sure," she said. "It looks like life's going pretty well for you right now, trapped between two delicious men, a large inheritance, and that beautiful face of yours." I heard a note of jealousy in her voice, though I could tell she was trying hard to smother it and be a good friend.

I shifted uncomfortably and gave Leanne a tight smile. These moments always made me feel guilty, like I was somehow not appreciating the hand I'd been dealt. But then the guilt always led to sadness. What was money without family? And what were beauty and men without love? Everything Leanne had mentioned was just a means to an end: happiness. And happiness had eluded me.

Leanne hadn't noticed my inner turmoil, yet she began to look concerned. "But you should know, he's a shapeshifter."

"Sorry—who?" I asked, still preoccupied with my

own thoughts.

"Caleb."

"Is that a bad thing?"

She shrugged, but I could tell she was holding back. "Not necessarily."

I came over to her and touched her on the shoulder. "Seriously Leanne, you should tell me if there's something I should know about Caleb."

She put down her makeup and sat on her bed. "Caleb as a person is fine. But shapeshifters are a scary type of supernatural." She still hadn't scared me off. After all, technically I was a scary supernatural.

She continued. "Lycanthropes and other were-animals can change into a single form, and their changes are dictated by the lunar cycle. Shapeshifters, however, can shift into various forms on whim. And the type of shapeshifter Caleb is, well, it's really rare. He can morph into any animal or person he wants."

I still didn't understand.

She took in my expression and elaborated. "He could hypothetically be in this room, right now. Literally a fly on the wall."

Now *that* was a troubling piece of information to hear.

Leanne continued. "With that kind of ability he's probably being recruited by the Politia."

"What's the Politia?"

"You probably don't know much about our government, The House of Keys, but when it was formed, a branch was created called the Politia, which focused on policing the improper use of supernatural power. This agency is still around, but it is extremely secretive. The Politia hires only the most talented supernaturals. I know that Caleb's father works for them, and I think that this agency is recruiting Caleb as well. Shapeshifters are incredibly useful to this police force since they can basically become anything or anyone."

"Why is this something I should be worried about?" I asked.

I could see she was trying to word her answer carefully. "The agency has been known to hunt things they believe are evil. And while there's been a truce for centuries, vampires are decidedly considered evil."

I looked at her skeptically. "So you think Caleb is going to off me tonight?" Then it dawned on me. "You think I've already been attacked by a shapeshifter—by Caleb."

"Of course not," she said. "The House of Keys has a truce with vampires. They do not kill rogue vampires so long as Andre deals with them." I swallowed. "And anyway, Caleb's not experienced enough to officially work for them. I was just thinking that his family probably wouldn't approve of the date."

"Well, thanks for the heads up."

So Caleb was a shapeshifter? I could already tell tonight was going to be fun.

I didn't see Caleb in my history class, which wasn't surprising considering all of his previous absences.

When I arrived in my anthropology class, Oliver was waiting for me, holding *The Beat*, the supernatural community's leading tabloid. He dropped the magazine on my desk. "You're getting cozy with your mentor and you didn't bother to tell me first?"

My eyebrows shot up. Splashed across the cover were pictures of Andre and me. One was from Mystique, clearly taken before I was attacked. Andre's expression was soft in the photo as he gazed down at me, and I was looking up at him, a secret smile on my face. Another was a grainy shot of the two of us embracing outside the French restaurant, and another the awful shot of Andre carrying me over his shoulder. The caption read:

LOVE AT LAST?

Andre's heating it up with Gabrielle Fiori,
the daughter of the deceased Count of Santo.
But is she the one, or will she get burned?

"Oh my—"

"You can say that again. At least your butt looks good."

"Oliver!" I swatted him with the magazine. He dodged me and slid into the desk behind me.

"But seriously G," he said, leaning over, "get used to this. The media loves him."

From where she sat three rows ahead of us, Doris turned around and scowled at us.

"Oh, go hump a tree Doris." Oliver rolled his eyes and began flipping through the magazine. Doris breathed in sharply at the insult before turning back around.

"Gabrielle, you haven't even seen the best photos of you two."

I groaned. "Can't wait."

Professor Blackmore cleared his throat, and the class quieted down. "Many of you and your parents have been concerned about the safety of school recently. Others of you have been the victims of violent circumstances," he said, looking directly at me. "So today and next week I want to center our discussion on classicism. What is it, when it was created, why it's been propagated throughout the centuries, and why academia has largely done nothing about it."

Andre had used the same word to describe one of my textbooks.

"Classicism is bigotry based on how genetically predisposed to evil someone is."

Outside the clouds had parted and the sun shone brightly into the room, bathing me and a few others in light.

"The flaw with this classification system is that it predetermines who and what is evil before the individual ever gets the chance to affirm or contradict the label."

I blinked as my eyes began to burn. I rubbed them and was surprised to find that my face felt hot.

"This is the model through which the supernatural community has viewed the world for the last two thousand years ..."

I could no longer concentrate. My skin felt like it was on fire, and my eyes were watering. I stood up, dizzy, and began walking down the aisle. Around me I heard gasps and whispers. Professor Blackmore paused in his lecture, looking concerned.

I pushed through the classroom door and ran to the bathroom. I went straight for the stalls and vomited. Weakly I walked over to the sink and held my hands under the water. Only then did I notice why my classmates gasped.

My arms were bright red. I looked up at my reflection. The sight was so startling that I staggered back. I was severely burned, my face red and swollen and my eyes bloodshot.

The sun had done this to me in under an hour. Which meant the stories were true—vampires couldn't be exposed to sunlight.

I shivered at the realization. I was a little less human than I was a week ago, and it was showing.

ꟸ ꟸ

After school got out for the day, I took a taxi to the International Bank of Man. Today I was going to find out what was in the safety deposit box that spooked Mr. Taylor.

When my turn in line came, I stepped up to the teller.

"Hello ma'am, how can I help you today?"

I placed the key I was given on the counter. "I need to close a safety deposit box today."

The woman stared at my key for a moment before looking back up. "Please follow me."

She walked me to a back office, where I waited until she returned with the safety deposit box.

She took my key and opened it. Looking vaguely bored she said, "It appears this was all that was left in the safety deposit box." She handed me a thin manila envelope. Written on the front was a single name: Gabrielle.

This was what was so urgent?

"If you need some alone time, feel free to stay here. I'll just be down the hall to finish your paperwork and close the account."

"Thanks, I'd appreciate that."

The teller inclined her head and backed out of the room.

I flipped over the letter and opened it. The sheet of paper I pulled out was already beginning to yellow.

Gabrielle,

If you are reading this then I am dead, and you are in grave danger. At the moment I write this I believe someone in the coven is preparing a political coup, and they appear to be targeting our family and Andre de Leon, the king of the vampires.

However, if you are reading this, then it also means that you survived into adulthood, and that Cecilia did her job and hid you well, something I can only hope for. I suspect that the betrayer, whoever he or she is, will tie up loose ends and attempt to kill you, regardless of whether or not Andre has been dealt with.

Do not believe you are safe simply because a decade has passed. That's the blink of an eye for a vampire, and we have the ability to hold grudges for centuries. My beautiful daughter, I must pass on this great burden to you—to find my killer before he finds you.

I don't have much relevant information for you to protect yourself with—only that this vampire is probably someone of high rank.

On the back of this letter I have written Cecilia's address. Find her. She is one of your greatest allies, and she will give you the answers you seek. Remember, people are almost never who they appear to be.

Lastly, never forget how much I love you. I know what loneliness feels like, and I suspect you now do too. I am more sorry than you can possibly know. I never meant to pass on that particular family trait. You are forever and always in my heart.

Dad

P.S. Speak of this to no one.

I reread the letter, holding onto the only written proof that my father loved me. Wiping away a couple stray tears, I focused on the more critical message. Political coup? That's what this was about? Why would I ever be a target? Andre I could understand, but me? I was too young and too ignorant to be significant.

Briefly I wondered if I was somehow vampire royalty—my father, after all, had been important—but the thought was too weird to hold onto. However, in general the idea that my lineage needed to be eradicated made sense—political coups often involved killing all members of the pre-existing ruling family. I just wasn't sure that my lineage was all that important.

Regardless, Andre clearly hadn't died, so what had happened?

My dad was correct in assuming that someone would try to kill me. However, the man that attacked me seemed to think I was an abomination. His attempt was more like a hate crime. It hardly fit with the motives of someone who wanted to overthrow a leader, and instead appeared to be more similar to the motives behind my mother's demise.

And Cecilia. The name clicked into place. She had been my nanny, the woman who helped me escape the night of the fire. The thought of seeing her again excited me, but I couldn't understand why she would be involved in vampire politics.

Now there were too many loose threads. I stared at the letter quizzically, trying to force together puzzle pieces that just weren't fitting.

I flipped the letter over and read Cecilia's address:

Cecilia Girari
Via Aldo Rollandi, 34
19010 Manarola, Province of La Spezia, Italy

My father said she had all the answers. I guess I was going to plan a trip to Italy.

Chapter 15

WHEN I GOT home, Oliver was waiting for me, munching on a stash of chocolates I always kept around.

He stood up, and a dozen little wrappers drifted off his lap and onto the floor. With the movement his skin shimmered, reminding me that he was otherworldly.

"You didn't tell me you had a hot date!"

I rolled my eyes. "As if it were newsworthy." I dropped my stuff next to the door and sat down next to Oliver on my bed. "So," I said, "how was your week? I haven't seen you for a while."

Oliver unwrapped another chocolate and shoved it in his mouth. "That's because you've been a hermit, and I've met the lust of my life!"

I raised my eyebrows and grabbed a chocolate. "Who is he?"

"His name's Rodrigo, and he's a Brazilian werewolf!"

I almost choked on the piece of chocolate I'd just popped into my mouth. A Brazilian werewolf? That sounded like a horrible wax job. Or a hideous hairdo. But definitely not an appropriate name for an object of lust.

Oliver contemplated his next chocolate. "He's just so gorgeous. Oh—and he's friends with Paul, my roommate. Apparently they went to boarding school together." Oliver's eyes lit up. "Maybe we could all grab dinner or something? That way I could be conveniently introduced without it seeming strange!"

"Ah. You haven't met him." I laughed. "Fine, set the date and I'll go. But only because I would never let a friend pass up the opportunity to officially meet the lust of his life."

"Oh my God!" Oliver grabbed my arm as another important thought came to him. "I'll take him to the autumn ball. It's in a month or so!" His eyes widened and he gasped. "You can take Andre. We'll be the cutest couples."

I let out a disgusted sound. "Not going—and definitely not with Andre."

"What? Of course you'll be going." He waved my statement away.

"Nope." I shook my head and plopped another

chocolate into my mouth. "I hate dances."

"You have to come."

I shook my head.

"Oh yeah? Well if you still have that attitude in a month, then that wicked little side of me that our textbooks thoroughly discuss will have to make an appearance."

I looked at him, trying not to laugh. "Are you threatening me?"

"You bet your knickers I am. I will not let you miss one of the best dances you'll ever go to because your little feminist heart has a problem with getting dressed up."

I stopped myself from rolling my eyes again. Bad habit of mine—along with eating chocolates and swearing. "What exactly are you planning to do if I don't go? Because, let's be honest Oliver, you don't exactly strike fear into my heart."

He smiled, and it was full of nefarious intentions. "I'll tell Andre you still have his blanket. And you sniff it every night."

My jaw dropped. I grabbed the decorative pillow next to me and wacked Oliver over the head. "I do not 'sniff' his blanket!"

"Ow!" Oliver smoothed his shirt out. "Harpy woman."

"How would you even contact him?" I asked.

Oliver looked offended. "I am a social media goddess. I have my ways. Just try me."

"Fine. I'll consider going." Heaven forbid Oliver tell Andre I sniffed his blanket. "But remember that you're to blame for the miserable time I'm going to have."

ꟷ

A half hour before I was supposed to meet up with Caleb, I threw on some black skinny jeans, a silky maroon shirt, and a pair of my knee-high boots.

After I put on a little mascara and a touch of eye shadow—my version of getting dressed up—I opened my laptop. I sent my mother a brief email. I'd increasingly had to censor myself when it came to communicating with her, something that made my head throb. We'd always been close, and omitting information felt a whole lot like lying to her.

Once I sent out the email, I pulled out my dad's letter and searched the Internet for Cecilia's address. When I couldn't dig up any information, I switched over to a virtual map. Google pinpointed the location, and I clicked on a satellite view.

My blood chilled as I stared at Cecilia's address. It was an open plot of land. Whatever was there had been condemned long ago.

"Girl, what are you doing?" Oliver sauntered over to my computer.

Immediately I exited out of the webpage before Oliver could see what I was looking at.

"Nothing." I swiveled in my chair to face him.

He took me in. "Tsk, tsk—you're not planning on going out looking like that, are you?"

"What's wrong with how I look?"

"You *are* going on a date, right?" I nodded. "Well, then you have to put some effort into getting ready."

"I have."

"Here, let me help—I'll be right back."

"Oliver—" I called out, but he ignored me and left the room. Five minutes later he came back with a bag of makeup in tow.

"Oliver, how did you get all of this?" I asked.

He brushed my question aside. "Paul is a conjurer, remember? Now hold still."

I let Oliver Barbie me up for the second time in two weeks. I had to admit, Oliver did a good job.

Once he was done, I looked in the mirror and saw someone who looked like me, only now all her striking features were amplified: bright blue eyes, red lips, pale skin, and prominent cheekbones, all surrounded by a halo of dark hair.

I briefly wondered what Andre would think if he saw me, and then mentally kicked myself. I didn't like him—even if the kiss we shared had been exquisite—and I didn't care what he thought. Just to prove a point I threw Andre's blanket from my bed into my closet.

My phone rang, and I snatched it up.

"Hey, I'm downstairs," Caleb said.

"Great, see you soon." I grabbed my purse and a coat and dashed past Oliver, who was sprawled out on Leanne's bed. He had moved on to eating Leanne's guacamole-flavored chips—specially shipped from the U.S.—and was watching some romantic comedy on her laptop.

"Bye!" he shouted, mouth full.

ꕤ ꕤ

I found Caleb leaning against the building when I came outside. He straightened up once he saw me. "Wow. You look ... amazing."

He might've been involved in my attempted murder. His charm was so disarming that I had to repeat this to myself.

"You clean up pretty well yourself." He managed to look both angelic and masculine—a tough combo to pull off—with his tan skin, blond hair, and those blue eyes.

"Well, I try." He smiled wide, his eyes crinkling. So misleading. Two, however, could play that game.

I smiled back eagerly. "I haven't seen you all week!" *Because you were missing school to learn how to kill me.* "I was worried you were going to cancel our plans." I pouted.

"Never!" He held out a hand. "Ready?"

"Where are we going?"

"It's a surprise."

"Fantastic." Just what my life was missing, surprises. Not.

ℬ ℭ

For once the surprise was actually something I enjoyed. Caleb took me to a zany fondue restaurant. Graffiti covered the walls, and all drinks came in glass baby bottles. We chatted about our boring professor, liking our classes, and living on the Isle of Man.

I remained suspicious of his true intentions, but talking to him was easy. And sadly enough, I liked the guy; it was too bad he and his family probably wanted me dead.

"So," he said after a lull in the conversation, "what's it like being a vampire?"

I looked up. "What do you mean?" Warning bells were going off inside my head.

He took in my expression. "Sorry, I wasn't trying to offend. The thing is, most of us grew up being told vampires were evil, bad—that if they weren't trying to steal your soul, they were trying to steal your blood and your life. It's a superstitious belief. We know that vampires do have souls and a code of ethics, but that fear has been passed down generation after generation. But you—you don't strike me as the 'evil' type."

"Whew," I said. "One down, only several thousand more to go."

He smiled, still waiting for my response.

I looked around the room. The noisy atmosphere covered up our conversation. I leaned in. "Being a vampire, or at least becoming one, doesn't feel like anything special. I have some heightened abilities, which make me feel like I've been colorblind my whole life. The sun has started to irritate my eyes and skin, so there's some discomfort. But other than that, I feel no different." I thought it best to hold back on the fact that fear and blood excited me, and that my new best "friend" was the king of vampires.

Caleb nodded, as if he had suspected this the entire time. He seemed so understanding. And then I thought back to the man who attacked me. It could've been Caleb or his father.

I interrupted his thoughts. "If I don't strike you as evil, then what *do* you think of me?"

I watched him closely, listening for an increased heart rate and any smells that would indicate he was lying.

"Honestly?"

I nodded.

"I think you're mysterious and sexy as hell."

My eyebrows shot up. Definitely not what I was expecting. His heart rate picked up, but he smelled normal—he wasn't lying. I looked at Caleb skeptically.

Because I didn't know how to respond to his statement, I turned his original question back on him. "What's it like being a shapeshifter?"

Now it was his turn to look surprised. "You know

I'm a shapeshifter?"

"What, trying to keep it a secret?" The edge was back in my voice. We were finally getting somewhere.

"No, it's not a secret. I just haven't told all that many people, and I didn't expect you to know."

"Oh I know *all* about shapeshifters—one tried to kill me a few nights ago." Technically, no one had *officially* said it was a shapeshifter, but I had to see his reaction.

His face went pale. "What did you say?"

I just stared at him.

His heart rate increased, and I could smell his nervous sweat. He was worried. Andre would be so proud of my sleuthing.

Caleb stood up. "I'm sorry, I have to go."

I opened my mouth, not sure if I had something to say.

He threw some bills on the table. "I'm sorry." He apologized one final time and left.

Well, I guess that explained that.

Chapter 16

I SELF-CONSCIOUSLY GRABBED my bag and left the fondue restaurant. The distance back to campus wasn't too far, maybe seven blocks, and the night was that perfect temperature that only occurs in the summer. I was glad I was alone. My dates had a tendency to end poorly, and I needed time alone to gather myself before I had to face Leanne and Oliver, who undoubtedly would want the scoop.

Damn siren genes. I bet they were responsible for my tendency to attract men and then rip them apart.

I turned onto the cobbled street that led to the campus grounds. A short distance away I could make out the remains of the Viking castle. From here Peel Castle was only a decayed, hollow shell. I now knew it was meant to trick the eye.

A thick fog rolled in from the ocean, and the blissful summer evening almost immediately transformed into a misty, cold one. I pulled my coat closer to me. The wet chill of the island seeped through my jacket surprisingly quickly.

The evening fog rushed inland from the ocean, gliding across the beach and over the small stone wall that separated it from the coastal road, before slithering down side streets. It looked like a living, breathing thing. I watched, transfixed, as it moved through the streets of Peel.

A cackle rose from the mist, and the hairs on my body stood on end. The most intuitive, primordial part of me knew that it was coming for me.

For a moment I was frozen, captivated and frightened by this force of nature. Then briefly, the fog thinned enough for me to see a man striding towards me.

The man in the suit. *Damn.*

The trance was broken, and I turned on my heel and sprinted towards my the dorms. My boots were heavy as I ran, and the ragged breaths I drew burned their way into my lungs. I really needed to run more often.

I passed through the campus gates. The dorms were less than a quarter mile away.

Behind me I heard another chilling cackle—much closer to me now—and I pumped my arms faster and pushed my legs harder. My building was rapidly coming closer. The doors were so tantalizingly close, yet it felt as though an ocean's worth of distance stood between them and me. My heart thumped heavily in my chest.

My ear tickled as someone whispered next to it. "Gabrielle ..."

I let out a choked scream and used the last of my adrenaline to push my body to the doors. I barreled into the hallway and crashed into Doris, taking us both down.

"Hey! What the hell? Get off of me!" Disgust curled her upper lip as she tried to push me off her.

"Did he follow me in?" I frantically looked back out the doors. Was it my imagination or did I hear faint laughter?

"God, you are such a freak!" Doris exclaimed. Belatedly I noticed the guy on duty in our lobby.

I got up, brushed myself off, and took a deep breath. I smiled at him, but fear and embarrassment made the corners of my lips waver. "Hi, uh, sorry about that. Someone was ... following me," I finished lamely. He eyed me like I was crazy. At this point, maybe I was.

I cleared my throat and said to Doris, "Thanks for cushioning my fall. That really would've hurt had you not been there." Her face flushed in anger. I decided sticking around was a bad idea and booked it up the stairs.

I staggered into my room.

"What happened to you?" Leanne asked at the same time Oliver said, "Looks like you had a *good* date, you frisky little thing!"

I pointed at Oliver. "Commentary not needed. And no, I did not have a good date."

I turned to Leanne. "Someone chased me," I said before I could stop myself. I bit my tongue before I mentioned that it was the man in the suit. Inwardly I cringed. My phantom was becoming bolder, and I didn't know how long I'd be able to keep my encounters a secret.

"What?" She looked shocked.

Oliver was still hung up on the date. "How can you fail two first dates in two weeks? You know that's really difficult. And by the way, you look like a wet dog."

My eyes shot daggers at Oliver, and Leanne chastised him. "How can you even talk about dates when someone followed Gabrielle home?"

"Well fine, look at me like I'm the bad guy."

Ignoring his comment, Leanne turned to me. "Are you okay? Were you hurt?"

"Other than tackling Doris on my way inside, I'm fine."

Leanne snickered. "That's what she gets for trying to seduce our freaking security guard. She's been down there for the past thirty minutes."

Leanne looked me over. "You sure you're okay? This is the second time that someone's been after you. We should report this. And where is Caleb? What an

A-hole, letting you walk home alone!"

I decided to sidestep the Caleb comment. "I didn't get a good look at the guy, so I'm not sure what use a report would do." I didn't want to go back to the police station and deal with them all over again, especially since there was no way they were going to find the man in the suit. I'd seen him disappear right before my eyes.

"Are you sure?" Leanne squinted at me.

I swallowed, shifting under her scrutiny. "I'm fine." The truth was that I wasn't fine. I hadn't been fine since I'd first seen him as a child, and it had only gotten worse as I got older.

Leanne didn't look convinced. "Really," I insisted. "I'm just going to lay low for the evening."

Leanne checked the time. "The party's going to start in an hour. You should come with us!"

"What party?" I asked. Normally I wouldn't even consider a party, but I didn't want to be alone tonight.

"The Seven Deadly Sins party! An alumni's hosting it off campus. I'm going as lust."

Oliver piped in. "She should be going as sloth. She's in denial."

"Look who's talking, Gluttony," Leanne said. "You blew through our entire stash of snacks."

Oliver put his hands on his hips. "I was hungry. And I was doing you two a favor. I saw you muffin-topping the other day Leanne."

I watched as Oliver got wacked by a pillow for the

second time today. It was becoming a habit. Leanne had a better arm on her than me, and she managed to lay Oliver out.

"Ohmigod, Oliver, I'm so sorry!" she cried.

Oliver pointed a finger at her from where he lay on the floor. "That's it. You're wrath."

ꕤ ꕤ

It took two hours to get ready, mostly because Oliver designed outfits for each of us and used his roommate, Paul, to conjure them.

Leanne did end up dressing as wrath, saying it made her look "fierce." Her deep maroon dress had convenient tears to illustrate her savagery—and her ample cleavage. Oliver made up her eyes in dark reds.

Oliver dressed as Envy. Only now as he wore an emerald tunic did I realize how regal he looked. His hair nearly reached his shoulders and looked so soft and silky it made me want to run my hands through it. His skin was luminescent; it sparkled and glowed in the dim light.

He really was going to make everyone envious, envious of his looks, envious that he wouldn't look twice at a girl, and envious that no man could hold his attention for long. I wondered if all fairies were like that—flittering from one person to the next.

Paul was "dressed" as pride; in reality he wore his usual clothes. Paul had begrudgingly decided to come to the party. I was guessing that Oliver had harped about it until Paul gave in. I could empathize; Oliver had beaten out nearly all of my resistance.

I eyed Leanne's outfit enviously. I wanted to look dangerous. Instead Oliver had insisted that I go as lust; I was going to look like a cute little sexbot, something I wasn't too happy about.

Oliver was huddled with Paul, discussing his drawings. Paul, who had looked bored designing Oliver's costume, had significantly perked up now that he was assessing the dress, and then me, and then the dress again.

I watched in awe as the dress materialized from nothing. According to Leanne, this type of conjuring—taking an idea and making it physically exist—was rare. Most conjurors could only duplicate an item physically in front of them. Apparently the Politica was looking into recruiting him. Big effing surprise; I'd hire him too if he could conjure my breakfast lunch and dinner.

And then Oliver held up the dress.

"*No.*" It was the skimpiest red dress I'd ever seen. The front had a plunging neckline and the entire back of the dress down to the skirt was bare save for a series of crisscrossing red ribbons.

I folded my arms. "I'm not wearing that skimpy thing. It looks like it went through a paper shredder. And why do I have to go as lust?"

"Because you are a siren—excuse me, the *last* siren.

And you're a vamp. I can think of no better definition of lust. And it's not skimpy; the skirt goes down to mid-thigh."

I huffed and puffed and lost yet another battle to Oliver. Reluctantly I put the dress on and was surprised to find that I looked good. Oliver touched up my makeup, making my lips a deep red color.

After we were all ready, we snuck out of the dorm, taking the damp underground passage. Apparently the staff and faculty did not approve of parties, so the persecution tunnels were really the only way to leave campus. So much for being considered an adult.

I heard a howl in the distance, and shivers raced up my back.

Oliver quietly swore. "These tunnels are so creepy."

"You can say that again." I rubbed my arms.

The party was exactly what I would have expected. We walked into a house and were met with the sound of a dozen different conversations, and distantly, the thrum of music. Everyone held bottles of beer or cups full of cheap mixed drinks. I watched a girl trip and stagger in her stilettos on one end of the room, while on the other end a college-aged guy kept up a slurred conversation with an uninterested girl.

But the most amazing phenomenon was that the alcohol brought out people's otherness. It was strange that I hadn't noticed it until now, but everyone had a slight shimmer to his or her form. The more intoxicated they were, the more prominent their otherness was.

A wereleopard woman had the trademark leopard spots along her exposed arms, and her feline face was superimposed on top of her human one. And another girl who must've been a fairy had her glittering wings unfurled.

"Dance floor!" Oliver squealed. I swear he had a radar for these things. He grabbed my hand and pulled, dragging me along with him.

I tried to make a grab for Leanne, but she stayed out of reach. "Nuh uh. I'm not dancing without first checking out the bar scene." She reached for Paul's hand and pulled him in the opposite direction.

The dance floor was in one of the house's larger rooms. Right as we entered, a nearly palpable wall of humidity assaulted us. I suppressed a shudder, knowing so many hot dancing bodies caused it. Almost immediately I began to sweat.

Techno music pounded, and I watched as shifting forms danced and glittered. I began to dance with Oliver, feeling incredibly awkward and uncomfortable. I tried to ignore the overpowering smell of sweat, body odor, alcohol, and urine. Hands snaked around my waist. I turned to find a guy behind me leering and gyrating. I pushed him away.

The humidity was making me dizzy, but I kept dancing alongside Oliver, determined that I just needed to loosen up.

A man stumbled past Oliver and me. I watched as

he clutched the wall before vomiting. The smell of it quickly overwhelmed my highly sensitive nose. And just like that, it was all too much.

I pushed through the crowd and left the room, Oliver calling out behind me. The air in the hallway was less humid, but no more refreshing.

"Gabrielle!" Leanne called from down the hall.

I came over to her. "I need to get the hell out of here."

"Agreed." She grabbed my hand. "They're all out of booze. How can they be out of booze? The night's barely begun!" I looked around the room at the very sloshed guests. The night was almost over for them.

We told the guys we were leaving and walked back to the dorms together. Leanne began telling me about the "loser" selkie—whatever that was—that tried to hit on her. "He was just looking for a good time, and I'm not that kind of woman." She flung her hair to the side. "I mean his home is in the sea! As if he's looking to 'get into a relationship.' Pssh, like I'm going to believe that."

Our dorm came into view. As we got closer, I felt a familiar rush of energy, and a figure slowly came into focus.

Andre leaned against the wall, arms crossed, watching me.

Leanne looked from one of us to the other. "Uh, I'll see you upstairs," she said to me. I watched her walk away.

"I heard you had a date." Andre's eyes roved over my itsy bitsy dress and heels.

"Is that why you're here?" I eyed him over. He wasn't showing any emotion.

He shook his head. "I was gone for a few days and I just got back." So that was why I hadn't seen him until now. "I wanted to see how you were doing. However, it sounds as though things are going just great for you," he finished.

Was he ... *jealous*?

I narrowed my eyes. "Frankly Andre, that's none of your business."

"Everything my subjects do is my business."

"Excuse me?" I said it quietly, but I was pissed.

He ran a shaky hand through his hair, a sure sign he was agitated. "Gabrielle—" He paused long enough that I wasn't sure he had anything more to say. His nostrils flared, and if I hadn't known any better, I'd say he looked pained as he spoke. "I'm sorry." He looked off at the ocean.

I furrowed my eyebrows. This Andre was nervous, and—dare I say it—*vulnerable*. I wasn't sure I liked it.

"I'm not sure what we have," I said, "but I wouldn't expect you to exclusively date me at this point." It hurt to admit this last part. The idea of Andre with another woman ... the mere thought was devastating.

I blew out a long breath. "Listen, if it makes you feel any better, the date was awful." Then again, Andre's and mine was also awful, so I wasn't sure that was comforting.

My words snapped him out of his thoughts. "I do not need to *feel better.*" He looked insulted. "And enough of this." He straightened up. "I didn't *just* come here to check on you. We have training, and tonight I am going to teach you the laws of being a vampire."

ꟹ ꟹ

We arrived at Bishopcourt a quarter till one. Like Peel Castle, candles flickered along the mansion's walls, throwing off both light and shadow. In between them hung oil paintings of various people in different eras of dress. The light played along their faces, making their frozen eyes dance and leaving me to wonder if they were still alive.

I followed Andre's sure strides until we arrived at his private quarters. I looked around at his antiquated office, which appeared to double as a library. Shelves of books filled the room. Behind a giant mahogany desk was a yellowed map of the world.

The room was an ode to history. Stacked on various shelves were clay and stone figurines, shrunken heads, carved animal masks, Egyptian stele, a collection of various ancient coins, and intricately carved weaponry. I stood there, mouth slack, taking in his collection.

He offered me a chair and sat across from me. "You like my office?"

"This is amazing. I feel like I entered Indiana Jones's office," I said, sitting down.

He shrugged. "When you live as long as I have, you inevitably garner a collection. I was actually thinking of redecorating."

"No," I said too quickly, and Andre raised an eyebrow. I cleared my throat. "What I meant to say was that I really like it, and I don't think you should change it."

He looked around the room, reassessing his office space as though he hadn't really seen it in a while. His eyes came back to mine. "We'll see."

He changed the subject. "I want to talk about some of the basics of being a vampire. There are three main rules. One, you are forbidden to change anyone into a vampire. Two, never drink to kill. And three, tell no one of who we are. Now—"

I interrupted him. "Uh, question. Doesn't everyone already know who and what we are?" I shifted in my seat. That electric thrum between us was stronger than ever, and I kept catching myself noticing things like Andre's silky hair or his strong jawline. Luckily he hadn't yet caught me ogling.

"Only the supernatural community knows our identity. But I am talking about the entire world. Humans have no idea we exist. Thanks to popular media, they believe we are simpering immortals who pine for true love. I'd like it to stay that way. That means no one can know we exist, and that also means drinking blood must be done privately—no witnesses."

"Ew."

He ignored my comment. "If rule one—never turn a person into a vampire—is broken, then it is punished by death. Unless the vampire has sired other vampires; in that case they're permanently incapacitated, since killing them would inadvertently end the lives of those they've sired.

"Rule two—never drink to kill—is not punishable by death unless it becomes habitual. Instead, punishment includes imprisonment and meals of animal blood." I made a face. I was going to have to get used to this drinking blood thing. "This rule can be difficult to follow because it is easy to accidently drink too much and thus kill a human."

"Have you ever killed anyone?" The second I asked it, I realized what a faux pas the question must be. Like asking an older woman her age.

His mouth thinned. "Yes."

Rationally I knew this, but thinking about it still made me squirm.

He watched me, in silence. I searched for something to say. I remembered my father's letter.

"My father left me a note in a safety deposit box," I said, sidestepping the current discussion. Despite Mr. Taylor's and my father's advice not to trust anyone, I thought Andre should know his life might be in danger. "He believed there was and still is a conspiracy to ... *remove* you—and possibly me—as part of a political coup. He wrote that we were both in danger."

Andre was quiet for a long moment, thinking over what I just said. "Santiago left this for you?"

I nodded.

Andre said, "At the end of his life, Santiago came to me and confessed that he had reason to believe there was a conspiracy to kill me. I did not think much of it at the time since the evidence was circumstantial, but after he died I became very careful. But months and then years passed and nothing happened.

"I will consider your father's words, but we both must remember they were written over ten years ago, and nothing has happened to me since."

Andre's words made me sad. I'll admit I agreed with him—the letter made no sense—but Santiago was my father, and I wanted him to be right.

"Why do you think Santiago thought I'd be in danger?"

He stared at his folded hands for a long time before looking back up at me. "Probably because you are related to him. And probably because he knew that after your powers were Awoken, you'd find me, making you a very visible target." He gave a small smile and looked at the clock. "I should probably get you home."

ည ထ

It was past 1:00 a.m. when we rolled up to my dorm building. I waved goodbye to Andre, watching his car—this time a sensible Audi—drive away.

I rubbed my eyes. God, I was so tired.

The wind carried a whiff of something—sweat? I heard a rapidly accelerating heartbeat and knew I had a split second to move.

I jumped out of the way as a man, intending to ambush me, flew past me. He rolled and was on his feet again.

I faced him off, frightened. Someone else was trying to kill me. This couldn't be coincidental.

My attacker shifted his weight from foot to foot, debating his next move. He was huge, but he smelled human. Then again, he could be another shapeshifter.

Belatedly I realized I was right in front of my dorm, where many people were peacefully sleeping. I let out a blood-curdling scream, hoping to wake someone up.

My attacker charged me, but he was clumsy. I sidestepped him and kicked his feet out from under him.

If I were paying better attention, I would've noticed the second heartbeat closing in on me. But I was so absorbed by my first attacker that I didn't until I saw the swing of an object in my peripherals a fraction of a second before it connected. There was a flash of excruciating pain, and then nothing.

Chapter 17

I WOKE UP in the back of a van, my head pounding. I tried to sit up, but my arms were restrained with duct tape, as were my legs.

Oh God. Where were we going? And what were they going to do to me?

The radio was on and an announcer was discussing a soccer game, each dip and rise of his voice making my already pounding head burst with new waves of pain. A foreign smell wafted over me, making me focus on the driver. He smelled like smoke and decay. Whatever he was, he wasn't human.

A metal grate separated me from the two men, so I couldn't get to them.

It was pretty clear they thought I was sufficiently incapacitated, leaving me back here to my own devices.

It was also clear that they weren't taking me to go get ice cream. If I wanted to live, I'd needed to act now while I still had the element of surprise. I knew that with a little effort I could break through the duct tape, and then it was a simple matter of jumping out of a moving car. I swallowed at the thought. The real trick was going to be staying quiet.

I tried pulling my wrists apart, but the duct tape wouldn't give. I tried again. Again, nothing happened. Luckily the idiots had bound my hands in front of me, so I brought my wrists to my lips and began to bite the tape. I tugged at it with my teeth, trying to rip an edge. Nothing. I bit down hard on the duct tape, now angry and panicked. I felt my canines elongate in response. *About time.*

I used my sharpened teeth to tear the tape. In order to remain quiet, I pulled the tape off agonizingly slowly, a layer of skin and hair peeling away with it. My eyes pricked with tears from the sharp pain and my pounding headache intensified.

I glanced at my captors. They were now cursing at some call the ref had made and the announcer was discussing.

I undid the tape that bound my feet slowly, glancing up again and again to make sure my captors weren't aware of my progress.

They must not realize how fast I heal. That, or they thought the blow to my head had mortally wounded me. Otherwise they'd keep a better eye on me.

Once I was free, I quietly slid to the back doors and tried the handle. Locked. I kept an eye out for my kidnappers, but they were still preoccupied with the game.

I took a deep breath for courage, and lay down along the floor. I pulled my foot back and aimed at the van's back doors. Putting all my strength into it, I kicked the door. The plastic crunched and metal creaked.

"What in the bloody hell?" One of the men up front turned in time to see me plant a second kick to the back doors.

"Stewie!" he yelled. "She's tryin' to escape! Grab yer fuckin' gun and shoot her!"

My third kick swung the door open. *Third time's the charm.*

I got onto my feet and prepared to jump. This was going to hurt. Behind me Stewie or the other goon cocked his gun.

I sent up a silent prayer to whoever was listening that I might survive this. I held my breath as my body left the van.

A shot exploded through the night air. The bullet hit my side before I touched the ground. I crumpled in midair and collided hard with the packed dirt of the road.

My body slammed into the ground, and I blacked out on impact. The pain consumed me.

When I came to several seconds later, all I felt was

pain. I lay there, unmoving, wishing I had stayed unconscious; the alternative hurt too much. The smell of blood made my nostrils flare, and through all the pain, I felt my elongated canines throb.

A short distance from where I lay, the van slammed on the breaks and pulled to the shoulder of the road. I watched both men get out, one with a gun and the other with a baton. I could tell they didn't see me right away. Neither had night vision. To them I was some dark shadow amongst other shadows.

I needed to get up, but everything hurt too much. Using my arms, I pulled my broken body to the side of the road. I bit back a whimper; the pain was unbearable.

"Hey Stewie, over there." The driver of the van pointed to me. I froze and let my body slacken. Perhaps they'd believe I was dead.

I heard gravel crunch as Stewie came over, gun focused on me. Through squinted eyes I watched as he stood over me, gun focused on my head.

"Tommy I think the bitch is dead." He kicked my side, and it was all I could do not to scream out. "Yeah, she ain't lookin' too pretty now."

His partner Tommy called out from somewhere in the distance. "Just put a bullet in her brain for good measure, and then let's get the body outta here."

"Did ya here dat princess?"

I had. And I'd be damned if I lived this long only to die at the hands of these scum.

Stewie cocked his gun, and I acted fast. I lashed out with my foot and kicked his feet out from under him. The gun went off, but the bullet missed me.

"What the—"

I crawled over to Stewie who was now on his back, and reached for the gun. Just as my hand closed over Stewie's, his shock wore off, and he began to fight back. I wrestled him for the weapon.

"Tommy, get over here! She's alive, and she's trying to get me gun!"

I heard Tommy's footfalls as he ran over. Panicked, I squeezed Stewie's hand as hard as I could, pulverizing bone.

He let out a blood-curdling shriek and reflexively let go to cradle his broken hand. I grabbed the gun and didn't pause to aim.

I pulled the trigger. The sound pierced the night, and Stewie went still.

Oh God, I killed someone. The hollow silence that followed the gunshot was so much worse than the noise.

Tommy stopped halfway over to me. "Stewie, is that you?"

"No." I aimed and fired. The bullet clipped Tommy in the shoulder. He cried out, staggering briefly. Then he sprinted to the car, clutching his arm, and I watched him drive away.

Sensing I was no longer in immediate danger, I slumped over and let myself slip into unconsciousness.

ഇ ര

At some point the blackness gave way to flashing lights and urgent voices. I looked around briefly before the vision faded away. I resurfaced again, just long enough to see faces leaning over me, and someone manually pumping oxygen into my mouth. I smelled so much blood. Then it too faded away.

The next time I woke up, I was in a hospital room. I listened to the monitors beep and whirl. My wrists were connected to all sorts of tubes. I moved to tug them off but immediately regretted it. Pain lacerated my body. I let out a small whimper as one of the monitors began beeping shrilly.

Immediately a few nurses came in to check on me, and a few minutes later my doctor followed. He smiled gently at me and pulled up a chair next to my bed.

"You're in here too often," he said. "How are you feeling?"

"Like road kill."

He chuckled and flipped through my chart. "You suffered some serious injuries. Two broken ribs, three more that are cracked, a gunshot wound, a compound fracture—your tibia—and a concussion." He paused to let me take it all in.

I could feel every one of those injuries. The damage must've been even worse when it happened, considering my quick healing abilities.

"I'm going to let you rest a little longer, and we

can discuss taking care of your injuries in the coming weeks and schedule a follow up." He got up and placed my chart in a slot on the door. "Get some rest," he advised in parting and closed the door behind him.

I took his advice and slept until I was roused by shouting outside my room. Between the yelling and the current of energy that had my heart rate hiking, I could hazard a guess at just who was outside my room.

The door burst open and Andre came storming through. He ran his eyes over my body, assessing me for damages. A nurse hurried in behind him. "Really sir, you need to leave."

He ignored her, and she cast a worried glance my way.

"It's fine," I said.

The nurse nodded, not looking convinced. "You get five minutes," she said to Andre, who wasn't listening, "and then you'll have to return to the waiting room." With that she turned and left.

Andre knelt close to the bed. "Who did this to you?" he demanded.

I managed to shrug without hurting anything too badly. "It doesn't matter. I ... I killed him—well, one of them at least." I closed my eyes and struggled to swallow down my bile. Even my throat hurt. The darkness behind my eyelids kept replaying the scene.

I opened my eyes. The anger on Andre's face had

drained away to concern. He looked me over, and I felt I might drown in the unexpected emotion I saw in his eyes.

"I heard."

The last thing I needed was for him to care, because if he cared, then the entire wall I had built between us might come crashing down.

I looked away from him and stared at nothing. "It was awful."

"I know. It always is," Andre said quietly.

"If I die, am I going to go to hell?" I didn't want to voice this question, but I couldn't stop myself.

Andre shook his head and smiled sadly. "I don't know—no one knows. But you're a good person, and you made the best decision you could—no one here would condemn you for what you did. And I'd hate to think God has less reason than humankind."

He took my hand and squeezed it. Even with the attack still fresh in my mind, my heart quickened at his touch. Out of the corner of my eye I saw Andre's lips twitch. He could hear my racing pulse.

What he couldn't hear were my racing thoughts. How beautiful he looked when he stared at me, and how he might be the first person I ever truly wanted to let into my world.

"I'm going to get you out of here," he said. "You're coming home with me."

ഇ ഏ

Thirty minutes later we were driving over to his place.

I glanced down at my jeans and shirt, both stretched tight over my various Velcro casts—which I'd be able to permanently remove in another hour or so. I was touched that Andre had actually gone to the trouble of picking up some clean clothes for me. If he hadn't, I would either be wearing a paper gown, or my bloodstained clothes from earlier this evening. I shuddered, remembering the events once again, and a wave of guilt and disgust washed over me. I had killed a man.

The car was silent for a long time while I pulled myself together. I took a deep breath. "I was ambushed," I said.

Andre looked over at me, brows furrowed.

I continued. "Right after you dropped me off, they were waiting for me."

Andre slammed on the brakes. I yelped as my seatbelt dug into my broken ribs.

"Are you okay?" Andre's voice sounded panicked. "I forgot you were hurt."

"I'm fine," I wheezed, trying not to pass out from the shockwaves of pain that ripped through my body. The guy really needed to stop doing that.

"You are *not* okay." He got out of the now idling car and came over to my side. After unbuckling my seatbelt, he lifted up my shirt to look at any additional damage he may have done to my ribs.

"Andre!" I said indignantly, pushing my shirt back

down. "I said I was fine."

"I was merely checking," he said. "I can be professional you know."

"Yeah right," I muttered.

He took my hands in his, ignoring my comment. "Now, you said you were ambushed right after I dropped you off?"

I nodded, trying to ignore how good Andre's touch felt.

He looked deep into my eyes. "From now on Gabrielle I am going to personally make sure this never happens again. Because maybe Santiago was right after all."

I was suddenly scared about the life I was living. Never before did I have to worry about things like assassins and political coups.

"Okay."

He stared at my lips like he wanted to kiss them, but he settled on kissing my hands. My heart fluttered before I could tell it to shut up.

Andre got back into his seat and revved the car up. He pulled the car out gently onto the road, careful not to hurt my broken ribs again.

"If Santiago was telling the truth, and someone is interested in getting rid of both you and me, then this tells us two things. The first is that you are the catalyst. Somehow your life has set these events into motion. It happened when you were a little girl, and it appears to be happening again now that the supernatural community knows you survived that fire.

"The second is that the madman may be interested in eradicating the entire vampire population of Europe."

Chapter 18

I STARED AT Andre for a few beats, letting the information soak in. "What do you mean by that?"

Andre gripped the steering wheel tighter. "I mean that I was the first vampire created ... I'm sure you've read about me in that textbook. All vampires are my descendants, meaning that I have directly or indirectly sired each and every one of them. My life may be the only thing keeping the entire population of vampires alive. And, although its never been tested, a popular theory is that if someone kills me, every vampire descended from me will die."

I didn't breath for a moment. "How many vampires have descended from you?"

"Hundreds. Essentially every vampire but you."

My brain was working, and a sick idea was beginning to form in my head. "You and me—the first vampire created and the first vampire born. They want to kill us because killing us would completely eradicate vampires."

A muscle in Andre's jaw jumped. "Yes."

⁂

When we pulled up to Bishopcourt, Andre attempted to carry me inside. I gave him an annoyed look and pushed his hands away. "Go away, I can take care of myself perfectly well."

"Fine." Andre crossed his arms and leaned against the car.

Of course, I had to eat my words as I tried to get my butt out of the world's lowest car. Stupid bucket seats.

"Still don't want any help?" He sounded so damn smug.

"No," I said, sulking. Slowly I pulled my broken body out of the car.

I saw Andre shake his head. I ignored him and began walking haltingly towards the palace. I stopped and leaned against the weathered stone. Everything hurt. Badly. Whatever healing powers I had weren't helping me very much.

Andre came over, arms folded. He looked down at me. "Do you want me to carry you, or would you prefer I pull out the wheelchair I now have to carry in my trunk?"

"Not the wheelchair."

He scooped me up and carried me inside to a guest room. I looked around at the room, feeling like I was in the midst of a fairytale. A large canopy bed occupied the center of the room. Billowy fabric was tied back at each of the four corners. The wallpaper depicted an enchanted forest. At the far side of the room, double doors opened onto a balcony.

He placed me on the bed and pulled up a chair to join me. "This room is always here for you if you need a place to stay." He slid my sling off of my shoulder but left my temporary casts alone.

"Why are you doing all of this for me?" I asked.

He furrowed his brows. "I'm your mentor. I thought you understood that, as such, I am expected to take care of you."

I watched him in the dim light, and suddenly his beauty was irresistible. Slowly I reached out and smoothed his brows. His eyes went soft. "But Andre, this is *way* above what I'd expect." I let my hand drop. "How many vampires *have* you mentored?"

His expressive face shut down, closing me off from his thoughts. After a moment he responded. "A few."

I fell back into the mound of pillows on the bed and laughed. "Oh-kay. That was an evasive response if I've ever heard one." I stared at the intricate molding on the ceiling. "I just wanted to know if you treated them all this well. Personally, I'd probably be a little jealous if someone came in and replaced me after all this special treatment." I laced my fingers behind my head.

"There is no way a vampire is behind these attacks—if that is what you are insinuating," Andre said. "My coven has protected me for seven hundred years; no one is willing to chance the death of hundreds to get to me. Especially not when death may or may not mean damnation.

"And now that you've been accepted into the coven, another vampire cannot kill you. *That* is an act punishable by death or permanent incapacitation. And trust me, death is what we vampires fear the most. No one would risk it out of jealousy."

It was my turn to raise my eyebrows. "I wasn't insinuating a vampire was behind the attacks." Strange that he'd jump to that conclusion.

"Now that we're on the subject, can you remember anything about your attackers?" Andre asked.

Hesitantly I thought about the two men who abducted me. "They both had guns and accents." I knew there was something I should be remembering.

"Oh!" I exclaimed. Andre raised an eyebrow. "One of my attackers smelled funny. Like smoke and decay."

Andre stilled. "A doppelganger came for you?"

I shrugged. I didn't know what the guy was. And I definitely didn't know what a doppelganger was.

He cursed to himself. To me, he explained, "Doppelgangers are considered to be shadows of a real person. They are dark creatures that feed off chaos and negativity."

"Sounds appropriate," I said.

Andre looked weary. "Doppelgangers are usually hired hitmen, and they are good. Whoever is behind this attack—and likely the one before it—appears to be increasingly desperate. Doppelgangers are expensive. Rarely do their victims escape." I didn't mention that the men appeared to be buffoons. I figured I'd get a little more street cred this way.

Andre was looking at me for too long. I felt my skin heat up and my cheeks flush, embarrassed that he could sense all of this. Slowly his eyes left mine, traveling down to my lips. I could see the conflict playing along his face: *to take advantage of the situation or to not?*

I heard his almost imperceptible sigh as he pulled away, retreating to his chair.

I snatched his hand as he turned and pulled him to me. Our lips met, and like fire the kiss consumed us. That familiar electricity ran between us, and I wondered if it would always be that way. His arm slid under me, pulling me close, and I could feel him pressed flush against me. I ran my hands through his silky hair, relishing him.

Never was I so aware of the way my body reacted to him, and how holding onto him felt like home. *I was falling for him.*

Slowly he pulled away, looking happily shocked.

Crap. What had I done? We could both hear my

rapidly beating heart. In contrast his remained as quiet as the day he died.

"I should let you rest," he said, backing towards the door. So he wasn't going to take advantage of the situation after all? From what I had heard about Andre, this seemed out of character. "Don't hesitate to call me if you need anything. I have two guards stationed outside, so nothing is going to get to you."

Those were some famous last words.

꙳ ꙳

"Gabrielle."

I woke to the sound of my name, not sure how long I'd been asleep. I looked around the room. It was still night outside.

I turned to go back asleep when I heard it again.

"Gabrielle."

My skin prickled. "Who's there?" I called. I sat up, now alert. A creak came from the far side of the room, and my head snapped in that direction. A figure stood outside on the balcony, cast in darkness.

My hair stood on end. I threw off my sheets and rushed towards the door to my room, determined to get the hell out of there and get help.

"I wouldn't do that if I were you." I stopped. I knew the voice that spoke to me. "After all, I'm a phantom that doesn't really exist, aren't I?" His voice tickled my ear.

I turned and stared at the man in the suit. He stood outside on the balcony, yet his voice whispered into my ear. He'd never gotten this close before, and never had he been so ... personable. If you could call it that. Gooseflesh blossomed along my skin.

"Let me prove to you that I am real." He smiled, and I reluctantly took a few steps towards him. Close up he was exceptionally handsome, and yet he exuded evil. You can't be attracted to someone who scares the hell out of you.

"You mean to say you aren't attracted to this?" He looking mockingly upset as he gestured to himself. "That's too bad. I was hoping you'd find me more to your liking." I stood there watching him just a few feet away on the other side of the glass, all my senses on alert.

"You don't need to be afraid of me. I can prove it." The balcony door unlocked itself and slowly swung open.

How did he do that? What was he?

The shadows gathered around him. "I am many things. You should know—you are many things as well." He stared into my eyes. "I hear you killed a man tonight—how delightful. We can add murderer to that list."

I broke eye contact and shuddered, disturbed by both his presence and the unwelcome reminder.

"Come with me." He held out his hand.

"No."

For the briefest of moments his friendly façade disappeared, and his face revealed intense anger. Then it smoothed over, back into his usual smirk. "If you do not come with me, then I will take you." Unwillingly, my eyes sought his out. I backed up, knowing he was serious.

For a heartbeat we stared at each other. Then I sprinted to the door.

He was on my heels in seconds, his laughter echoing along the walls. He grabbed me, and I only had time to scream before a true and terrible darkness descended.

Chapter 19

BRIGHT MORNING RAYS woke me. I sat up, knowing something wasn't right. I glanced about my bedroom. Leanne was already gone. At the foot of my bed was a newspaper.

I picked it up. "Victim, Villain or Hero? Violent Attack Leaves One Perpetrator Dead and Another Injured." Scribbled over the story in sharpie was a note: *When you get this, find me. We need to talk!* I skimmed the story; my name was splashed throughout it.

In a rush the entire evening came back to me, ending with the man in the suit.

He took me. I shoved my fist in my mouth to stifle my scream. My skin crawled. I had no memory of the time between then and now.

I scrambled out of bed, and then paused when I realized my casts were gone. When had they come off? And *who* had taken them off? At least nothing hurt too bad; my injuries were almost entirely healed.

I grabbed my phone from my bag.

19 missed calls. 8 voicemails.

I clicked to see the details. The majority of the calls were from Andre, but the most recent were from Caleb, Leanne, and Oliver.

As I clicked through my numbers, Leanne came in.

"Where have you been!" she exclaimed. "I just got back from the hospital. They said you left last night."

"You mean I wasn't here when you woke up?" I asked.

"Of course not! When you didn't come home I figured you were with Andre. But after I read the morning newspaper, I realized something was majorly wrong. I rushed to the hospital to find you. They told me you'd checked out last night."

I felt my heart stop. I'd been gone for hours.

"I did check out," I replied, "and I was with Andre."

My face must've betrayed my calm response because Leanne crossed her arms and leaned on our wall. "Listen girl, are you okay? What's going on? This is the second time someone has tried to kill you—technically the third, if you count that guy who chased you."

I looked up at her and willed her to believe me. "I'm fine—a little shaken up, but fine." What I couldn't tell her was that *that guy who chased me* had subsequently abducted me.

"Okay, if you say so." Leanne wasn't buying it, not for a moment. But with a final skeptical look, she grabbed her towel and left to take a shower.

I looked down at the phone still clutched in my hand. More than anything, I wanted to hear the messages Andre left. I put the phone to my ear and listened to my voicemails.

The first message was from right after I was hospitalized. Andre had left a message saying he was on his way to pick me up. I skipped to the next message, also from Andre.

"Gabrielle, the guards said they heard you scream. I'm outside your door now, and I'm coming in."

The line was silent as Andre opened the door. I waited for him to get back on the line, but the silence stretched on. Finally he found his voice.

"Cristo! What happened? She's gone!" His voice was panicked.

Andre yelled to someone, *"Secure the perimeter. We're going to need to review all footage and check every room."*

Into the phone, he added, *"Don't die on me."*

The following three messages from Andre told me nothing important about what happened.

I rubbed my eyes. Either I was insane and I blacked out, removed my casts, and walked home, or I had just spent the night and morning with the scariest man I'd ever met.

The sun must've risen in the time between Andre's messages and the three from my friends that followed. Theirs, unlike Andre's, were only concerned about the attack from the night before. That meant that Andre didn't tell them about my abduction.

I left a message for Andre that I was safe, and that I couldn't remember the night's final events. He wouldn't receive it until he woke up this evening, but at least this way he'd know I was okay. Then I fell back onto my bed.

A deep, despairing fear possessed me. I didn't think I was crazy. But accepting that meant I had to confront something even more chilling: whoever the man in the suit was, he was powerful and interested in me. And now he was unafraid of making contact.

When I went to put my phone back in my bag, I noticed a golden slip of paper between my notebooks. Where had it come from? I thought back to one of the first times I'd been in the library, reading the book on sirens. It could've been the same piece of paper that had fallen out of the library book.

I went to throw the paper in the trash, when black calligraphy caught my eye.

G

Alone within a crowded room
You have felt the breath of doom

Your predicament a result of fate
Seek me out before it's too late

C

The hairs along my arm stood on edge. *My initial is just a coincidence*. It had to be, or else Lydia, the librarian, had passed along a note. The idea seemed so remote and implausible that I tried to shake it. I flipped the paper over.

Nona's Bed and Breakfast, Cinque Terre, Italy

Below it was a vaguely familiar address. I went to the computer and Googled the name and address. The first hit matched the strange card, so I clicked the link. I perused through the images, all of the beautiful bed and breakfast and the coastal town it was situated within.

Just as I was considering leaving the site, I absent-mindedly clicked the "About" tab. The paper slipped from my fingers.

Cecilia.

ꟷ ꟷ

I sat in Peel Castle's library, reading a textbook and waiting for the sun to set so that I could talk to Andre.

My thoughts kept drifting from my supernatural anthropology book to last night's events and then the cryptic note I'd found. What was so shocking about the note was the possibility that Cecilia was both aware of my existence and trying to make contact with me. And Lydia mediated that contact.

I briefly considered confronting Lydia, but something told me that she'd deny involvement. I jotted down a quick note to book a flight to Italy. I think a reunion with my childhood nanny was long overdue.

I glanced out the window before turning back to my reading. The school grounds were awash in blue and periwinkle hues as the sun dipped below the horizon. Not five minutes after sunset my phone rang.

"Hello?" I whispered, packing up my bags. I got the stink eye from a girl sitting a few seats down.

"What the hell happened last night?" I could practically see Andre running a hand through his hair. "Are you hurt?"

"No I'm fine." I glanced around at the people studying. They looked bored, and I wished I could be any one of them. My life no longer had a shred of normalcy. "Like I said in my message, I can't remember anything."

"How did this happen? Bishopcourt is impenetrable, and nothing was caught on camera."

I remembered the man's words from last night: *I'm a phantom that doesn't really exist, aren't I?*

"Where are you?" he demanded. "I'm picking you up right now."

We ended up meeting back at my dorm room after

he batted his eyelashes to this evening's security monitor and slipped her a little under-the-table cash.

"Apparently if I don't watch over you all the time, you're going to get killed or maimed." He was stalking back and forth in my tiny room, looking like a caged panther. "So from now on, I'm going to be watching you throughout the entire evening."

"Excuse me?" He had to be kidding. I couldn't deal with Andre for that long.

"This is non-negotiable," he said. "I'm not going to argue with you."

My eye began to twitch. I hated being bossed around, even if it was on behalf of my safety. "Well, sorry to burst your bubble," I said casually, "but you won't be able to watch me *every* evening."

His expression was haughty. "And why is that?"

"I'm going to be out of the country in the next few days. I already booked the flight for next weekend." It was a white lie, but only until I got the chance to jump on the Internet and book a flight.

"Where are you going?" He was suddenly much too close. "And why have you not cleared it with me? You must clear all travel arrangements with me first."

"Puh-lease Andre," I said, pushing him back to a more appropriate distance. "I don't have to clear personal travel with you. Plus I'll probably be safer out of the country."

He came in close, once again invading my personal space. He was distracting at this distance, with his high cheekbones, strong jaw, and expressive eyes, and the electricity between us was almost overwhelming. "You're not. You're not safe away from me."

I rolled my eyes. He was one wrong comment away from me losing it.

He continued. "No one will attack you so long as you're with me. I'm coming with you."

"Andre, no. This is about my father. It's personal."

"If I remember correctly, we were both mentioned in his letter. That means this includes me."

I hesitated, thinking over his words and trying to find a good counter argument. Andre could see my momentary acquiescence, and he moved on it. "Great. Forget about your ticket. We'll take my jet."

My jaw slackened. "No—"

"There is one thing you have not mentioned," Andre interrupted. He searched my face. "Who kidnapped you?"

"I don't know." I shrugged, attempting nonchalance. How was I supposed to explain the man in a suit?

Andre studied me. "You're lying." He rubbed his chin and looked out the window. "But why?" he asked, more to himself than to me. He turned to me. "Are you protecting someone? Perhaps a lover?" I could tell it bugged him to say that.

"Ugh, no Andre. That's sick." I cringed. The thought of intimacy with the man in the suit was nauseating.

I sighed, taking a seat on my bed. "Last night I was taken by someone who I've known for my entire life."

Andre sat down in my computer chair, dwarfing it. He looked as though he was prepared to listen.

"I really don't know much about who he is—I don't even know his name—but I don't think he's involved in any plot to kill me. He's haunted me for as long as I can remember. And he followed me here, to the Isle of Man."

I looked at Andre, wondering if he believed a word I'd said. I wouldn't. But, judging by his expression, he seemed to.

"He's followed you your entire life? Have you ever mentioned this to anyone?" The corners of his eyes were strained, worried.

I shook my head. "Who'd believe me?" Hesitantly I looked into his eyes, and I'm sure he saw the vulnerability laid bare in my own. "I'd always assumed he was a hallucination. Last night was the first time he actually made physical contact."

Andre's foot began jiggling, and he ran a hand through his hair. "I believe you," he said quietly. "But I'm hoping he's not who I think he is. How *did* he abduct you?"

I concentrated on my pile of textbooks sitting on the desk. "I woke up when I heard him calling my name. He was out on the balcony." I sighed. "He appears and disappears at will. And he makes himself known only to me, even when others are present."

I thought back to my twelfth birthday. He had stood outside on my front patio, next to my adoptive mom and a neighbor who she was chatting with, both oblivious to his presence. "I don't know how he does it, or why he's so powerful. Most of all, I don't know why he has chosen to haunt me."

Chapter 20

THE NEXT DAY as I sat waiting for history to begin, Caleb made a beeline for the seat next to me. I stifled a groan. Not another problem to deal with. I had enough on my plate already.

He dropped his bags, slid into his chair, and leaned towards me. "Hey," he said hesitantly, "I heard about the attack. Are you okay?"

"Yeah I'm fine," I said, twirling the pencil in my hand.

"I heard you were hurt pretty badly," he said, eyeing my unblemished skin.

I shrugged. "I heal quickly. No big deal." I was a big, fat liar. It was a big deal, and I was still shaken up by it. I really hoped he wouldn't ask about the guy

I killed. That was a subject I couldn't pretend to be cavalier about.

He studied me, then sighed and rubbed his face with his hands.

"Hey, are you okay?" I asked.

He leaned over his desk, resting his head in his hand. "No. Absolutely not. First I learn that a shape-shifter attacked you. Then, I make the idiotic mistake of leaving you to seek the answers out for myself, and someone else tries to kill you."

Innocent. Caleb was desperately innocent. Even if I didn't have supernatural abilities I'd come to this same conclusion. He was blaming himself for my attacks.

I let out my breath. "Listen Caleb, I already have one overbearing man in my life who feels personally responsible for my well-being," I said, thinking of Andre. I reached out and touched his arm. "Please don't join him. I could really just use a friend right now."

He looked down at my hand and then up at me. "Of course," he said, "I'll always be your friend. And I promise I will make this up to you somehow," he said, gaze intense.

I tried to lighten the mood. "Well in that case, I have some history homework I'm behind on ..."

He laughed, his smile brightening his face. "Bring it on!"

One suspect cleared. Only a few hundred more to go.

༄ ༄

That night Andre brought me back to Bishopcourt to continue my training. Now more than ever he felt it was important for me to know the extent of my powers.

This time when we arrived at the mansion, we wordlessly passed by the waiting entourage.

Theodore met us inside. His eyes briefly flicked to me before they turned their attention back to Andre. "Sir, the king of Jordan is on the phone—"

"Tell him I'll call him back." Andre didn't even pause midstride.

Theodore scowled at me, clearly blaming me for Andre's cavalier attitude. "Andre, it's important."

Andre halted and met Theodore's gaze. "It can wait." His tone indicated that there was no room for discussion. Turning to me he said, "Follow me."

We walked up an ornate set of stairs to the back of the mansion. This was further inside than I'd ever been, and the farther we walked, the older the decorations became. A series of antique atlases lined the walls, strange sea monsters and ships decorating the painted ocean. The portraits back here were old, some nearly unrecognizable with age.

We passed an encased hand, and I shuddered.

"Saint's relic," Andre said in answer.

"People collect those things?" I wanted to gag.

"Some of my people thought it might bring us closer to salvation."

"Did it?"

Andre paused to look back at me; his expression said it all.

"Right. I'm guessing that's a no."

We turned another corner that faced a large, solid oak door. Andre twisted the brass knob and held the door open.

My breath caught as I walked in. Much like his VIP suite, the room was full of rich colors. Gold-patterned cloth covered the walls. An ornate tapestry hung high above us on one wall. Another wall was entirely composed of books. In the middle of the room stood a ridiculously large four-poster bed.

But what caught my eye was the painting. It hung behind the bed. A much younger—and yet identical—Andre sat in chain mail, wearing the sign of the cross. He'd been a crusader.

"Another attempt at bringing myself closer to salvation," he said, noticing my interest.

"I'm guessing that didn't end well?"

Andre contemplated my statement. "Bringing me closer to God? Definitely not. There's nothing holy about killing another human, no matter what god you believe in. However, I was well fed during the Crusades. That much I can say about war."

I glanced back at the painting. "Your eyes ..." I trailed off. Nothing more needed to be said. Whoever had painted Andre's portrait had captured his anguish perfectly. This was not a triumphant man, but a broken one.

Andre came up next to me. "I keep it up to remind myself of my humanity. I wasn't long a vampire when this portrait was commissioned, so my horrors still weighed on my conscience. Now it's hard to remember how remorse and guilt feel."

He turned from the painting to face me. "Now, let's talk about your training."

I eyed my surroundings. "Uh, we're in your room."

"I thought you'd want some privacy for what we're about to do next."

My heart rate escalated, and a warm flush crept up my neck and cheeks. The energy between us was suddenly everywhere, and I was very aware of how good Andre smelled.

"Wh—what are we about to do?"

Andre walked towards me, a slow smile spreading across his face. Heat pooled in my belly, and I thought I might melt. Instinctively I backed up. My brain told me that I didn't like where this was going, but every other part of me told it to shut up.

My back hit the wall behind me, and then there was nowhere else to go. Andre didn't stop until his torso was flush with mine. He ran a hand past my jaw and cradled my head. His expression was tender.

Hesitantly his eyes traveled to my neck, and I knew exactly what *we* were about to do. And, so help me, I was perfectly fine with it. He opened his mouth, and

I caught a rare glimpse of Andre's fangs.

Slowly Andre let go of me and backed away, his fangs receding back into his gums, and I blinked as if waking from a dream. "Captivating your prey. That's what our lesson will be about today. How to convince a human to willingly give you their blood."

"Did you—did you just emotionally screw with me?" My voice was quiet, but I was anything but calm.

"I was demonstrating how you—"

I crossed the room faster than most people could blink and I punched him in the shoulder. Andre barely reacted to the punch.

"*Shit!*" I grabbed my fist; it was like punching stone. "Don't you *ever* mess with my mind again!" I said between clenched teeth. He'd toyed with my emotions, and I'd fallen for it.

Andre merely watched me, clearly waiting for me to finish. "Don't give me that look," I said. Inwardly I cringed. I sounded just like my mom. "It's not like someone was messing with *your* head."

"First, I wasn't messing with your head. Those were pheromones. While normally vampires don't have natural scents, we can produce pheromones in large quantities when we're hunting." I made a face. "And second," he said, ignoring my expression, "stop complaining. You get to do the same thing to me."

"I do?"

"Yes, and try not to look too excited; it makes me nervous."

I smiled devilishly. "A chance to exact my revenge? Of course I'm excited."

Now I understood the need for privacy. It would be a little hard to focus when other people were milling about. And now that I was focused on payback rather than seduction, I was all too willing to participate—maybe this had been Andre's strategy all along.

"So what do I do?"

"Convince me that I want to give you my blood."

"How do I do that?" I asked.

"You have to will it. It's as simple as pushing the thought out into the world. Speak the words over in your mind until I respond," Andre said from where he leaned against one of the bedposts.

"Wait," I said as a couple thoughts struck me at once, "aren't other vampires immune to that stuff? And won't I suck at this—I'm still mostly human."

Andre straightened and took my hands. "True, you probably won't be able to do much since you are mostly human. But you still need to practice because eventually you won't be human, and this technique is how vampires survive.

"And yes, I'm immune, which makes me better at gauging how well you're doing."

"So, no revenge?" Now that my motivating factor, successfully captivating Andre, had been removed, the exercise seemed pointless. How disappointing.

"I didn't say that. I'm ready to be convinced."

"Hmph." I collected myself. Best to get this over

with.

I began to think about convincing Andre. *You want to come closer. Come closer.*

This is so dumb. I had to bite my cheek not to laugh at how ridiculous the situation was.

"I'm not convinced at all," the peanut gallery said from where he leaned against the bedpost.

His taunt irritated me; I was determined to captivate him if only to wipe that smug look off of his face.

A rush of energy surged within me. My fingers tingled, and I felt something dark and exciting stir.

Get on the bed. I blinked at the command. Who wanted to get beds involved? Surely that wasn't me?

Slowly Andre backed onto the bed, never looking away from me. He smiled, indicating he was still in control. I, however, wasn't so sure he was, and I wasn't so sure I was either.

Again I felt my skin tingle, and my back arched as something rose up within me. What was this strange power? This couldn't be how I captivated prey. Andre would've warned me about this.

I stretched as something inside me uncurled itself. My skin softly glowed, but I barely noticed. Andre had my whole attention.

I walked to the bed slowly, rolling my shoulders back and smiling seductively. I'd never done this before, but somehow I knew what to do.

Andre stilled. "Gabrielle?"

I didn't answer him. Instead I crawled onto the bed,

slowly making my way up to the headboard, Andre's body beneath me the entire time.

Andre's eyes changed as he stared at me. I'd never recognized the look in his eyes as resistance before, but now I knew because he finally let his guard down. He must've been resisting a great many impulses when it came to me.

His eyelids dropped, and the look he gave me was pure heat. He brought his hands to the sides of my shoulders. "Gabrielle ..."

I kissed his cheek, his stubble convincing me he was not nearly so dead as everyone believed.

He pulled the edge of my shirt over a shoulder and rose to kiss the exposed flesh. I grabbed the bottom of the black shirt he wore and tugged. He helped me, and together we removed it.

I sat, staring at his tan, sculpted torso. Both me and the creature inside me were mesmerized by nothing more than beautiful male anatomy. I wasn't sure how long I sat there, staring at his chest before the magic receded, and I was left to pick up the pieces.

For a second time this evening I blinked away my confusion. At least now Andre shook it off as well.

"What ... did I do?" I asked, mortified to find myself straddling Andre, my top askew and his missing. In an instant I was off the bed, pacing.

Andre, for his part, managed to look troubled and satisfied at the same time. He lounged on the bed, arms behind his head, not bothering to put his shirt back on. "Well, you managed to seduce me, for one."

"What was that!" I cried. I felt icky, as though someone else had possessed my body.

"I think we've discovered the siren inside you."

"That *thing* that possessed me was a siren?"

"Nothing possessed you. That was all you; it's just another power that you need to learn to control."

"I never want to learn to control that," I said vehemently. "That thing was destructive."

Andre put his shirt back on. "Well, you won't need to learn how to captivate your prey since you can use glamour."

"What does this mean for me?" I asked fearfully. Would I try to seduce everyone I wanted to munch on?

Andre frowned. "I don't know."

There was one thing I did know: the king of vampires was not immune to it.

ꙮ ꙮ

Shortly after sunset Friday evening, Andre and I boarded his jet and headed to Italy. It was time to talk with the last missing piece of the puzzle that was my childhood.

A little after midnight we landed at a small airport in Cinque Terre. A sports car waited for us a short distance away.

"This is the way to live," I commented. "No lines,

no waiting." There was even a man ready to open the passenger door for me.

"You mean to tell me there's another way to live?" Andre grinned as we got into the car. Behind us Andre's minions—excuse me, his entourage—got into two black Mercedes.

I rolled my eyes, even as I smiled. Cocky bastard. "You know, arrogance is not an attractive quality in a man."

"That's not what the ladies tell me." He winked as he gunned the engine, and we took off.

The town sat along the edge of a cliff, lit by twinkling city lights. The warm evening breeze washed over me as we drove along the coast's edge. I'd almost forgotten that it technically was still summer. The chilly climate of the Isle of Man made it difficult to wear a T-shirt and jeans even in early September.

We pulled up to a grandiose house that Andre had rented. I went inside, tugging along my suitcase. "Choose whichever room you desire," Andre called out behind me.

Lavish was an understatement. Diamond cut crystal vases were scattered throughout the entrance hall and living room, each overflowing with flowers. Oil paintings hung along the walls.

I chose a room with a balcony overlooking the water—I'd be damned if a phantom scared me out of the best room in the house.

I sensed Andre behind me without hearing him enter. "Are you sure you want to stay in this room?" he asked, nodding towards the balcony.

"Yeah." I faced Andre, my breath catching as I took him in. I realized now it wasn't just his raw attractiveness that drew me to him. There was also something mysterious and sorrowful about him. He'd seen over a half millennia of history unfold, and at times like this I could see it in his eyes.

Oblivious to my thoughts, he came over and gazed out at the ocean. "Strange to think that the last time I was in this city with your father was during World War One." My skin prickled at the thought.

With a shake of his head, he looked at me, and the old, wise Andre was gone, replaced by the fun-loving man I knew so well. "So, what do you want to do? I'm free for the rest of the night."

I groaned. "I was thinking of going to bed."

"Nonsense." He looked at me, his expression amused. "You are such a strange creature. You're supposed to be changing into a vampire, yet you want to go to bed at midnight." Andre said the word mockingly. He took my hand. "I have another lesson to teach you."

"Ugh. Can't it wait?"

"For what, you to die?"

I fell silent. I had no good comeback.

"There's an additional incentive: afterwards we'll do something fun."

We ended up on the beach. With my night vision,

the beach and ocean were a deep and brilliant blue.

"So what's the lesson?" I asked.

I sat down next to Andre on a blanket we had brought along, our shoulders touching.

"This," he said, staring out at the ocean. "Civilizations rise and fall, people live and die, times change, but not the ocean. It's the one thing that remains constant."

I breathed in the salty sea air. "I've always loved the ocean. Now I understand it's my siren genes that make me long to be close to the water."

Andre pushed his hair back, watching the waves. "Not everything boils down to a matter of your identity." He looked over at me. "Speaking of change, have you noticed anything different about your abilities since your Awakening?"

I shook my head. "Other than the sun irritating my eyes and skin, and my heightened senses, nothing has progressed." I picked up a pebble and threw it at the crashing surf. The pebble shot out of my hand, traveling far and fast out into the ocean. "Andre, why do you care so much about me? And don't tell me it's because you're my mentor." I looked at him inquisitively.

He was quiet for a long time. Finally he spoke. "I don't know." He ran a hand through his hair. "The truth is that since the moment I saw you across the club, I haven't been able to stop thinking about you."

We could both hear my heart accelerate—yet again.

He continued. "At first I thought it was the chase that attracted me. It was intriguing and frustrating that you weren't interested in me." He gave me a devilish smile.

"Then I tried to convince myself that it was because you were Santiago's daughter, and I wanted to honor our friendship and protect his child. But—" he leaned in and pushed back my windswept hair, "each time you were attacked, I panicked."

He cupped my face. He looked at me like I was beloved. "There are no words to describe what I am feeling. I cannot remember feeling this way. Ever."

This was crazy. He ate humans for breakfast. Not to mention he was older than Father Time. So why was I falling for him, falling for him when I couldn't help but push everyone else away? It frightened me to feel this way, yet I couldn't stop this and didn't want to.

Slowly, so slowly, he leaned in. My lips met his, and that fire between us ignited again. The current of energy pulsed through us, alighting my skin.

I fell back onto the blanket, pulling Andre down with me. He pressed himself even closer to me, and hesitantly he ran a hand along my face and neck before making his way lower. I gasped as he cupped my breast. No one had ever touched me that way.

He flashed me a pirate smile, and my breath caught. God, he was sexy.

I tried to tug his shirt off, but he gently took my hand and whispered in my ear, "Not tonight."

I began to pull away, hurt by the rejection. He groaned and tightened his grip as he caught my gaze. "You don't know how hard this is for me." His eyes flicked to my neck. "All I want is to explore every inch of you and not let you go until I've thoroughly satisfied us both." My breathing sped up at his words.

He slid his hand up my neck until he cradled my head. "But I don't want to rush this—rush you. Because I'm planning on sticking around for forever, and if I sabotage this now by rushing you, I'll never forgive myself."

The pounding of my heart hit a crescendo. And then, the world stilled, just like it had the first time I saw Andre.

I love him.

There it was. The truth I'd been burying ever since I laid eyes on him. Because I didn't believe in love at first sight, or that anyone could see past my face. But most of all, I was afraid that if I let someone in, I'd lose them, just like I had my family.

"What if I don't want to wait?" I asked, breathless. Somewhere in the back of my mind, the prudish Gabrielle wanted to take this slow. But my realization and the heat between us had consumed me.

He searched my face, unaware of my thoughts. "You might not want to wait right now, but once you are alone in your bed tonight, you will, I promise." He leaned in and kissed me deeply. "And I don't want you to regret anything when it comes to this."

I wanted to open my mouth and argue, but I knew from his tone that I wouldn't sway him tonight.

So we lay there as the waves rushed in and out, hands touching and mouths lingering, but nothing more.

At some point later I could see the sky subtly lightening. "Now it's late." Andre's husky voice tickled my skin as he kissed my jaw. Regretfully I disentangled myself. He grabbed the blanket and we walked back. His hand reached for mine, and I took it shyly.

He left me at the door of my room, kissing me one last time. "All I'll be thinking about until this evening is you." I blushed—blushed—at his words. "Remember to wait to talk to Cecilia until I wake."

"Yeah, yeah," I said, smiling. "Night." I closed the door, and after changing into my pajamas, slipped into bed.

I couldn't stop smiling. I think they call this giddiness. Who knew I was capable of it?

ꙮ ꙮ

When I woke up, it was four in the afternoon.

I swore. The entire day practically passed me by. If I wanted to see Cecilia alone, I had to move fast. I grabbed the first shirt and pants I saw in my suitcase. Running to the bathroom, I quickly brushed my teeth and shook out my loosely curled hair.

It was hard to explain why it was important I visit

Cecilia by myself, but I felt that this reunion was too personal for witnesses. I also didn't want to bombard Cecilia with our presence.

I wrote a brief note explaining where I was going, and that I did not get kidnapped, killed, or maimed.

I pulled out Cecilia's address and slid it into my purse. Now came the tricky part.

Four human bodyguards had come along with us, and they had been given explicit instructions to follow me wherever I went. Somehow I had to get by them undetected. I listened at my door. I could hear at least three separate voices chatting in the living room. There was no way I could slip out the door without them seeing me.

I walked out onto my balcony and looked down. I was on the second floor. If I climbed over the railing and hung from the bottom of it, I would only have a few feet to fall. Easy.

Yeah, right.

I swung my legs over, and slowly lowered my body until I only hung onto the wrought iron balcony by my hands. Taking in a breath, I let go. The drop was a lot farther than I had imagined, and my knees stung from the shock of my fall. I shook it off, pulled on my shades, and hailed a cab.

A half hour later I stood outside Cecilia's beautiful bed and breakfast. As I stood in front of the villa, I suddenly worried my presence was not wanted.

I summoned my courage, and before I could chicken out, walked through the door.

I entered a homey living room. Sitting on the couch across from me was the woman who raised me the first few years of my life. She'd been arranging a collection of magazines on the sitting room's coffee table, but looked up when the door opened.

"*Buon giorno* ..." Her voice trailed away as her eyes widened. "Gabrielle?" Cecilia covered her mouth.

I wrung my hands together and smiled nervously. "Hi Cecilia."

Cecilia looked as though she hadn't aged a day since we last parted. "Come here *tesoro*," she said, the Italian endearment rolling off her tongue the same way it used to when I was little.

She set her magazine aside, stood up, and approached me, arms open wide. We embraced, and I could feel her wet tears soak into my shirt. "I knew you'd eventually find me."

She pulled away and patted my cheek. "My, my, how beautiful you are. You are all your mother." She laughed light-heartedly.

"You knew my mother?"

"Of course," she said. "Come my dear, you look hungry. Let's go to the kitchen; it appears we have some catching up to do."

I followed Cecilia into the kitchen. Sheer lace curtains hung from the windows. A shelf of wines hung from one of the walls, as did a string of garlic.

"Please sit," Cecilia said, indicating to the table.

She pulled out a tray of cookies and poured us each a cup of tea.

I was so nervous I didn't think I'd have an appetite, but once I saw the cookies and smelled the tea, I remembered how hungry I was.

Cecilia sat down across from me and patted my hand. "We have a lot to talk about."

It took about a minute to adjust to my surroundings. Cecilia was alive, sitting right in front of me, her dark hair, olive skin, and almond eyes evoking such a bittersweet emotion—why had she left me all those years ago?

I let out a breath. The truth was that I had so many questions I didn't know where to start. "I was brought here by a letter my father left for me."

Cecilia's eyes widened for a moment. Then she nodded. "Santiago feared for your life, so he fixed his will, wrote that letter, and gave me instructions on what was to happen to you if he died. I was to take you far away and hide you in an orphanage.

"I thought that an orphanage was perhaps the most awful place for you to go, so initially I wouldn't agree to it. But in the end, it really was the only way for you to go undetected. He had your birth certificate forged—"

My eyes nearly popped out of my head. "You mean to tell me that March twenty-third is not my real birthday?"

She shook her head. "Your real birthday is December eighteenth. You are actually three months older than what your certificate says." She looked questioningly at me. "You don't remember this?"

I was speechless for a moment. I'd been celebrating the wrong birthday and didn't even realize it? Finally I collected myself. "No," I said, "I don't remember that at all. I don't have many memories from before the fire." I was still reeling from that bombshell. "… So, then is my real name Gabrielle Fiori?"

Cecilia smiled kindly. "Yes. That should've been changed too, but Santiago wanted you to keep some part of him.

"I'm so sorry," she said sincerely, patting my hand. "Your father loved you so much. He was positive that whomever was after him would kill you as well. That's why he went to such great lengths to hide you. He wanted to make sure that no one would discover you. If he had it his way, you'd still be in Los Angeles, oblivious of who you really were. He felt that was the only way you'd avoid the tangled mess he was in, and the siren's curse."

Belatedly something she said clicked. "You didn't want me to be a part of the supernatural community?"

"That's right."

"I assumed you were the one that told Peel Academy of my existence." My head was hurting. Why weren't these pieces of my life fitting together?

Her eyes looked sad. "My dear, I have no idea who did that. Someone must've figured out your identity.

I thought we were thorough," she shrugged, "but I guess we weren't thorough enough." That was a riddle for another time.

Outside the sinking sun seemed ominous. My time was nearly up. I needed some answers. "Cecilia, two people have already tried to kill me." My voice shook. "Do you have any idea who's behind the attacks? My dad's letter said you could help."

She looked out the window. Her eyes were distant as she spoke. "I saw the attacks in the paper, and I read about your attackers. It could be anyone—the House of Keys, a hate group, or perhaps individuals acting independently. But," she said, turning back to me, "I think it's most likely an insider. A vampire. No hate group is that persistent, and the House of Keys would be more discreet—and more successful."

"No, that cannot be," I said, immediately rejecting her theory. There was one obvious flaw. "It can't be a vampire. They wouldn't risk killing themselves as well as rest of the vampire population. Andre said so himself."

"Andre?" Cecilia looked frightened. "You should trust him the least."

"What?" Why was she acting this way? "He's helped me since my Awakening."

Cecilia crossed herself. "That long ago fire? Other than your family and me, Andre was the only vampire who knew the location of Santiago's safe house, the same house you were raised in and that burned to the ground. Your father trusted him, but I fear he put his faith in the wrong man."

My heart plummeted. Dread flooded my system, and my pulse beat loudly in my ears. That couldn't be true. *Please let it not be true.*

Dizzy from the adrenaline and the awful tightening in my stomach, I barely managed to voice my next question. "But why would Andre try to kill me?"

"My guess? Because you were born a vampire, and that calls into question the very foundation of his authority."

"That seems unlikely."

"Not when you're quite comfortable with killing humans."

The only sound in the room was the rhythmic ticking of the clock on the wall. I sat there, trying to comprehend her words.

Had last night been a lie? Nausea rolled through my stomach at the thought. I trusted him. And he might've played me this entire time. I almost had sex with him.

I begged myself not to cry.

"So, you think Andre killed my father? And now he's trying to kill me?" I held my breath.

She sighed. "I don't know. But even if he wasn't responsible, he's not completely innocent. Just be careful."

Too late for that.

Andre might be trying to kill me. The realization

finally sunk in, and it felt worse than dying. Worse than getting stabbed or shot. It felt like betrayal.

But could I trust Cecilia? I didn't want to. My heart screamed that she must be lying. It was easy to jump to the conclusion that Andre was guilty. He'd already admitted to me that he'd killed before. But hell, I'd killed someone as well; that didn't mean I'd do it in cold blood. What made Cecilia innocent?

"Please don't take this the wrong way," I said, "but why did my father choose you to hide me?"

She considered my words. "One, because I was random," she said. "No one would guess the nanny could wield that kind of power. And two—and more importantly—because he trusted me completely. He knew what I was."

"What are you?" I asked, looking out at the twilight sky.

She smiled. "I am a fate."

Chapter 21

WHY DID I never make the right choices when it came to men? Why did I have to let Andre in? These thoughts ran through my mind as I sat in the taxi heading to the airport.

My body felt weary and my heart hurt. The sadness tugged at the corners of my eyes and mouth, pulling them down.

Once I left Cecilia's, I'd called a taxi and booked a flight back to the Isle of Man through my phone. I couldn't go back to Andre. Not now after what I learned.

I'd tried so hard my entire life to keep people at arm's length, and when I finally let someone in, he ended up being a prime suspect in my attacks.

Just my luck.

The sadness and betrayal welled up in me, and I let myself cry, not caring that the taxi driver could hear my sobs.

How had I not considered it before now? Every time I'd been attacked he'd just left my presence. In retrospect it now seemed obviously coordinated.

Pulling myself together, I leaned my head against the window, letting my breath fog up the glass. I had to face the possibility that I had fallen for and stayed with my father's killer and the person behind my own attacks.

But why would he try to kill me? What threat could I possibly be? He'd already introduced me to the coven. More importantly, why *hadn't* he already killed me if that was his plan? It didn't add up.

My body shook as I watched the scenery fly by. Last night came back to me, and I began crying all over again. I couldn't erase my feelings for him. I could've sworn the look in his eyes last night was genuine. I could've sworn his concern was genuine. But he'd had so many years to perfect the art of lying.

My phone rang for the fifth time. I didn't need to look at the caller ID to know who was calling.

I turned off my phone and wiped my cheeks. How would I protect myself from him? Andre was everywhere and nearly all-powerful.

I watched my tears dampen the armrest. Maybe everything was a lie, and Andre was innocent. But for the time being, I had to take Cecilia's warning seriously until the attacks stopped. I was going to have to stop seeing Andre.

ꟹ ꟹ

Throughout the plane ride I analyzed my talk with Cecilia over and over again, trying to understand whether Andre really could be pretending to like me while trying to kill me.

My thoughts felt clinically detached. I'd folded my heart up and stowed it away since it'd only gotten me into trouble. I would approach this logically from here on out.

Grabbing my textbook from my bag, I flipped to the page on the fates.

Known in Greek mythology as Moirai and in Roman mythology as Parcae, the fates were three sisters who were the incarnation of destiny. Clotho spun the thread of life; Lachesis measured the length of the thread of life; and Atropos cut the thread of life, choosing the time and manner of each person's death.

I read through the passage until I came to the final useful piece of information.

Few people have ever encountered the fates, so very little is known about them. What is known is that they will only reveal themselves to those deemed worthy.

Now I understood why my father trusted Cecilia and why I should too. If you had destiny working for you, your odds were pretty favorable.

I bid goodbye to my budding relationship and breathed in and out. I was strong; I'd get through this as I had all other calamities.

As I put the book away, one thought lingered: what was a fate doing as my nanny?

so cs

When I arrived on the Isle of Man early the following morning, it was drizzling; the heavens reflected my mood. I shivered as I walked outside the small airport in nothing but yesterday's T-shirt and jeans. Because I hadn't gone back to Andre's villa after Cecilia's warning, I had nothing with me except for my book bag. Luckily it contained my wallet and cellphone, but I'd left behind my suitcase.

I hailed down a taxi and came back to Peel defeated. I'd lost Andre and was still no closer to understanding who was after me, or why. The only good the trip had done was remind me that I could trust no one, not even the one man who I'd actually let in.

I opened the door to my dorm, and once I was inside, collapsed against it. Then I let it all out. The tears of frustration, betrayal, and dashed hopes. Couldn't I just be a normal girl for once?

"Bitch please."

My head snapped up. Oliver was lounging on my bed, eating more chocolates and flipping through a magazine.

"Don't even go there," he said without looking.

I felt my cheeks heat. I gave him a look that could curdle milk, but he didn't even have the decency to glance up. "What would you know about my life that I don't?"

He guffawed. "You're crying because you're having man troubles—obviously. And you need a reality check."

"For your information, I already received one. Considering that my *man troubles* might also be responsible for the attacks on my life."

Oliver closed the magazine and walked over to me. "Do you know this for certain?"

"No."

"So you're *worried* that Andre's behind your attacks. Pardon me for saying so, but those aren't angry, pissed off tears running down your cheeks," Oliver said, pointing to my cheeks. I put a hand to my face. "Those are the tears of an angst-y teenage girl depressed over a broken relationship.

"Someone's trying to kill you—Andre or not—and this is what you're worried about? Please, you have worse problems."

Oliver rendered me speechless. He had said the rudest, most hurtful, and most brutally honest thing I'd ever heard.

"Leanne's freaking out," he said. "Despite her reliable abilities as a seer, which *foresaw* otherwise, she thinks you're dead. But I knew you weren't—you're a survivor. So while she's running off her stress, I decided to wait for you to show."

"Has anyone told you that you are a mean little fairy?"

"Oh, no one's told me *that*. The boys have always told me I'm a big, rowdy—"

"Oliver!" I threw my purse at him, which he gracefully dodged.

The door to my dorm jiggled a second before opening. A wet and panting Leanne came in. Her jaw slackened when she saw me.

"Told you," Oliver said.

She pointed a finger at me and between gulps of air said, "Stop doing this to me. You're going to kill me with all the stress."

Immediately I felt guilty. "You're right. I'm sorry—I should've called."

"So what *did* happen if you didn't die?"

I spent the next fifteen minutes filling Leanne and Oliver in on my trip, including my make-out session with Andre, and the possibility that world's oldest vampire might be trying to kill me.

For a moment, the room was silent, and then Leanne cleared her throat. "You met a fate? I didn't even think they were real. What was a fate doing as your nanny?"

I glanced at our rain-splattered windows. "That's what I want to know."

ꙮ ꙮ

The next day in History, I began jotting down notes on what I knew about my past and the attacks. Andre was the prime suspect, but I wouldn't let my feelings cloud my sleuthing skills. After all, someone else could be responsible. I didn't have many hard facts.

As usual, Caleb was absent. In the background, Professor Mead droned on. "The *Glashtyn* is a water horse who appears as a dark and astoundingly handsome man only distinguishable by his pointed horse ears. In all folktales he captures or attempts to capture women—"

A voice boomed through the room. "Gabrielle Fiori, Principal Hazard requests your presence."

You have got to be kidding me. Thirty different heads swiveled in my direction.

I made my way out of the classroom. From memory I traced my way back to Principal Hazard's office. Beyond his open office door he leaned over a scattered pile of papers. I knocked, standing in the doorway.

He glanced up. "Oh, Miss Fiori. Come in, come in." He beckoned me over. Unceremoniously I dropped my bag and coat on the floor and took a seat across from Hazard.

I folded my arms together and lounged back in the

chair, annoyed and letting it show. "I haven't done anything to Doris, so what is this about?"

"Well, Miss Fiori," he said, flustered by my gruff manner, "you certainly have not done anything wrong." He loosely folded his hands on the desk. I could literally smell the waves of distaste coming off of him. He might have said I'd done nothing wrong, but he thought otherwise.

"However," he continued, "the school is worried that with the multiple attempts on your life, your presence poses a threat to other students. Especially after the second attack occurred within campus grounds."

I raised my eyebrows. "What are you saying?"

Principal Hazard looked uneasy. And guilty. "Miss Fiori, we cannot endanger the entire student body because of your situation."

"Let me try to understand this better. You've determined that, because there have been multiple attempts on my life, *I*, the victim, am a threat to other students?"

"Miss Fiori, you must think of the other parties involved here. Innocent students. Your presence puts them in jeopardy."

"So, are you kicking me out of Peel?" I fixed my gaze on a bust of Pallas Athena that sat on a shelf behind him.

"No, no. We are putting you on independent study. You can come and go into the school and use all the facilities outside regular hours. You will, however, need to find an alternative place to stay. ... Perhaps your leader will be *accommodating.*" My nostrils flared as I took in his disgust.

I stood up, shaking from head to foot. "Please," I implored, "make an exception. Andre might be the one who's trying to kill me."

Principal Hazard shook his head, his withered skin flapping. "I'm sorry. I cannot."

All the willpower that had kept me going left, and my body sagged in on itself. "How long do I have until this comes into effect?"

"Independent study will begin tomorrow, and you have until Sunday to find a place to stay. I'd suggest discussing this week's assignments with your teachers so you can stay on schedule."

"And what will happen when my attacker is captured?"

Hazard stared intensely at me for a few long moments. "Everything will go back to the way it was."

I forced myself to smile. "Great. I look forward to it." He frowned, his creases deepening.

Without another word I grabbed my bag off the ground and headed for the door. It was as I walked out of his office that I smelled it.

Hatred.

❧ ☙

I left the study halls of Peel Castle around 8:00 p.m.

I'd spent a good portion of the afternoon thinking of how I was going to find my attacker, bring him—or her—to justice, and manage to stay alive, all in under one week. Three hours later and no closer to solutions, I decided to pack up and head home.

Outside, rain was coming down in torrents. Dang. I'd forgotten to bring my umbrella this morning. The walk across campus to my dorms was a good hundred yards, so there was no way I'd make it back dry. I just hoped the notes inside my bag didn't get wet.

As I got closer to my dorms, a figure came into focus, somewhat obscured by the downpour. Andre.

He stood out in the rain, drenched from head to toe. He hadn't even bothered to try to keep himself dry. Too bad the look suited him so well, the moisture giving his face a healthy sheen and the water dripping from his hair making him all the more wildly sexy. I was sure I looked like a drowned rat.

I was tempted to turn around and walk back to Peel Castle. But just as soon as the thought crossed my mind, his gaze captured mine. My heart thumped a little faster, and I tried to convince myself that it was because I was scared and not because of how much I still achingly loved him.

He wasn't going to attack me here—that much was certain. Too many potential witnesses.

I walked up to him. "So you found me."

He ran a hand through his hair, his tell. He was anxious or—more likely—annoyed. "I'm not even going to go into all the ways you could've been hurt leaving like you did."

I gave him a look. Overbearing much?

"So I'll just ask you why—why did you leave? What did I do to push you away?" The hurt in his eyes constricted my heart. I was expecting a whole lot of anger, but not this. Perhaps I had it all wrong.

But how could I know? A guy wasn't worth risking my life over ... even one that I had fallen for—hard.

"This is all happening so fast," I lied, using our budding romance as the excuse. "I think I need some distance."

His mouth thinned, and he looked grim. "That's what you want? Even with your attacker still at large?"

"Yes."

He stared at me for a long time before speaking. "Fine," he said eventually. "I'll give you your distance, and I'll leave you alone. But I will have around-the-clock security watching over you—"

"Andre—"

He put a hand up. "No." His voice was hard, and for the first time I felt his coldness, his distance. *He* was pushing *me* away. "I think we can both agree I've been exceptionally lenient,"—true, at least for Andre's standards—"so this is non-negotiable.

"Lastly," he looked across the campus, "there's a gala at the mansion on Saturday—for my birthday of all things—I hope you'll come. It starts at eight."

For a moment I forgot my problems. "You're having

a *birthday party?*"

He looked chagrined.

I held up my hands. "I'm sorry. It just seems so … normal."

He shrugged and glanced at his watch. "I have to get going. Just promise me you'll stay safe." His eyes were intense.

I was wrong about Andre. I had to be. "I promise."

"Call me if you get nervous or just need to talk. I'll be waiting." He turned and walked to his car. I watched as he got in and drove away, feeling like mistrusting him was a big mistake.

୨ ୧

When I walked into my dorm room, Leanne and Oliver were watching funny videos on my bed, as if the world had not shifted on its axis. I'd avoided coming back here this evening for this very reason. I'd have to tell them about my visit with Principal Hazard—eventually.

"Hey gorgeous!" Oliver said around a mouthful of chocolate. How much chocolate could I possibly have left by now? "Come join us!" He scooted over to make room for me, a huge feat for Oliver.

My throat constricted. I'd lose this in a week. All because someone was trying to kill me. Sometimes life just wasn't fair.

ꕤ ꕤ

I yawned as I flipped the page of my textbook that Friday evening. My eyes blurred as I tried to read about early Viking settlements on the Isle of Man.

It was one of the lamest Fridays I'd had in a while, sitting in the library, catching up on my reading. However, following my conversation with Principal Hazard, I'd decided out of spite that I would do all my homework inside the castle. This way if I was attacked, it increased the chances that the castle would also get maimed. Petty, but possibly effective.

I hadn't even considered looking for housing. Nor had I told Oliver and Leanne about having to move off campus, though they knew about independent study. Instead I'd spent the week scribbling notes in my notebook, trying to determine who my attacker was and why he or she was trying to kill me. My sleuthing skills had still gotten me nowhere.

I stretched and looked around. I jolted when I realized I was alone. Somehow I managed to outlast even the most academic of my peers. Pulling out my phone, I checked the time.

"Crap, eleven-thirty?" I hadn't meant to stay this long. I packed up my bags and put on my coat.

As I grabbed my bag, I heard a rustle from the far side of the library. I froze, listening.

When I was certain no one was there, I walked past the rows of musty, leather-bound books, their embossed covers shimmering gold in the low lamplight of the library.

Just as I left the library I heard it again: a rustle coming from somewhere behind me. I hurried my pace, determined to get out of the spooky old castle. It was eerie here at night.

The candlelight flickered in the wall sconces, making the light dance along the rough stone walls. Behind me I heard a growl.

I turned. An enormous black dog with glowing red eyes stood in front of the library doors I'd exited not a minute before. The Moddey Dhoo, according Professor Mead.

Great. *That* was a true legend?

The dog's hackles rose and it barred its teeth. Saliva dripped onto the floor, where it sizzled away. It inched towards me.

"Good doggy," I said, edging backwards. The exit was down the next hall. With my speed I could probably outrun the dog. Only, I had no idea what I was dealing with. Demonic dogs weren't really my forte.

It growled louder, and it began to pace back and forth, agitated. I saw the dog pause and its muscles tense. Then it charged me.

I turned on my heel and sprinted for my life. I could hear its paws clicking on the stone floors behind me. Some phantom dog—that thing sounded real to me.

I flew down the hall, barely losing momentum to turn the corner. At the end of the hall was the exit. Behind me the Moddey Dhoo snarled. It sounded much too close.

Putting in one last burst of energy, I plunged through the exit. I glanced behind me in time to see the dog jump through the solid oak doors.

I swore. I'd really hoped the dog would stay inside the castle.

In front of me was Peel Castle's expansive lawn. Wisps of fog obscured the far side of the campus where my dorm was. I ran blindly in that direction.

Through my pants I felt the dog's hot breath. It was right on my heels. My muscles protested as I forced them to move faster.

I didn't slow down until the dog's growl became a distant noise. I glanced back. The Moddey Dhoo stood in the middle of the grassy lawn, staring calmly at me. As I watched, the dog slowly faded.

I shivered as its glowing eyes finally winked out. The dog was an omen of death.

This time I was in deep.

ꟷ

"Kill me. Please." Leanne moaned when I woke her up the next morning. "That would be the kind thing to do."

Her and Oliver hadn't come home until the wee hours of the morning, so I hadn't had a chance to mention my encounter with the ghostly dog.

"Want something to eat?" I asked, holding up the bag of pastries I'd bought an hour earlier, a peace offering in case she didn't like being woken up.

I'd barely touched my own breakfast. I had been anxious all morning about seeing the Moddey Dhoo, even going so far as to research what I knew about the demonic dog. It was more of the same: the dog was an omen of death.

She sat up in bed. "Sure, what'd you get?" she asked, scrubbing her face with her hands. I handed the bag to her and watched as she pulled out a Danish and began to nibble it.

I took a tasteless bite of my croissant. "Leanne, I have something to tell you."

"What?" she asked, yawning.

"I saw the Moddey Dhoo last night." I glanced up from my plate to watch her reaction.

She stared off in the distance. Then, slowly, she looked at me. "You saw ... ?" She trailed off, "But that's impossible," she said. "The only people that see the Moddey Dhoo—"

"Die. I know."

Her gaze sharpened on me. "Let me give you a reading."

I raised my eyebrows. "But I thought you just *saw* stuff."

She rolled her eyes. "Yes, I foresee things, but it's more accurate if I give you a reading." She reached out. "Here, give me your hand."

I put down my croissant and gave her my hand. She closed her eyes and took a few calming breaths in and out. All was still for a few minutes.

Suddenly, her hand tightened over mine, and her eyes darted back and forth behind her closed lids.

"I see a mansion. People are wearing formal attire." Could she be talking about Andre's birthday gala?

Leanne's fingers dug into mine. "There's a fire. Trapped. So many people trapped. All of it burning down. I see you. I see Andre, and a gun, aimed at you. The trigger is pulled and ..."

She let out a muffled moan and dropped my hand. Hesitantly she opened her eyes. They were red.

"Gabrielle," she said, "you will die if you go to this event."

Chapter 22

THE SILENCE THAT followed sounded louder in my ears than a scream.

"What exactly is it you're going to?" Leanne asked.

"Andre's birthday party."

Understanding broke out along Leanne's face. "Right before you died I saw Andre and a gun."

I felt lightheaded. *Andre's going to kill me.*

I didn't think my heart could break anymore, but I was wrong. Even after Cecilia's warning, I'd carried around the secret hope that he was innocent.

My chest ached, and my stomach churned painfully. How could people live like this? Why would anyone want to fall in love? This was awful.

I blinked a few times to push back my tears and met

Leanne's shocked gaze.

I had a decision to make: go and die, or stay and ... probably die in the near future. Leanne's vision also indicated that I had to come to terms with the fact Andre was playing me.

I felt my conflicting emotions resolve themselves. "I'm going. I have to." I nodded to myself. I had to save those people.

Leanne looked at me as if I were insane. "You can't. You'll die. I *saw* it."

"Leanne, people will die whether or not I'm there. You said yourself that the guests were trapped in the burning building. We know this will happen. I can evacuate them if given the chance."

She took this in. Then she nodded. "Fine. But I'm going too."

Now it was my turn to look at her like she was crazy. "No way. I can't let you risk your safety."

"I'm not letting my friend walk to her death without some backup."

"Leanne!"

"I've already decided. You can't change my mind. I'm coming."

The door burst open to reveal a shirtless Oliver. "Oh. My. God." He was wide-eyed. "When did I get a bellybutton piercing?" He gazed, horrified, at the pink and clear crystals dangling from his navel.

"Pixie dust." Leanne shook her head. "You tried pixie dust last night, and then decided to get your bellybutton pierced."

If I'd been in a better mood, I would've laughed. Instead I said, forlorn, "I wish I could've been there."

Oliver glanced up, his gaze piercing. "Is everything okay, G?" Somehow, he knew. He knew that my heart was broken, and he knew that only one thing could've caused that.

Leanne met my eyes before she turned to Oliver. "We think Andre's planning on killing Gabrielle tonight at some party." I felt a tightness in my chest as she spoke the words out loud. "Gabrielle, however, is still planning on going so she can save all the others I foresaw die. So now I'm going with her."

"No—" I began.

Oliver pulled up a chair and sat down next to us. "In that case, count me in."

"No." I rubbed my temples. "Please. I don't want either of you getting hurt."

Oliver scratched his chin. "If I remember correctly, I am the bossy one in this relationship, not you. So, I'm coming."

I sighed, looking at the clock. It was 3:00 p.m. "The gala starts at seven. That means we have less than four hours to come up with a plan and get ready."

Oliver squealed. "I'm designing our outfits!"

ꙮ ꙮ

It was while Oliver was pinning up Leanne's hair that

I heard a knock. I got up and opened the door.

I balked at the visitor. "Caleb?"

He scratched the back of his head nervously. "Hey."

"What are you doing here?"

"I texted him," Leanne said. Oliver eyed him up and down like he was a juicy morsel. "I thought he might want to help."

I squinted at Leanne. After his apology last week, I knew Caleb would've eagerly assisted us tonight. But I hadn't told Leanne about Caleb's apology. So why had she contacted him?

I swallowed. Whatever she saw must've been awful enough that she called in a favor. That, or he was in the vision.

I looked back at him. "Did Leanne tell you what you're getting yourself into?"

"Enough to know the danger."

"And you still want to do this?"

Caleb pushed past me and ambled in. Awfully presumptuous of him. He was looking at a glass paperweight of mine when he answered. "I've been in training for this type of thing for years."

"I'm not sure I understand," I said.

He glanced up and our eyes locked. "And I'm not sure I'm authorized to tell you ... yet. Just trust me when I say that I'm prepared."

"Okay," I blew out my breath, "then let's get you suited up."

ꕥ ꕥ

At 7:30 p.m. our taxi pulled up and we dashed inside. "Where to?" our driver asked.

"The Bishopcourt mansion," I said. "And I will double you're your fee if you can get us there as quickly as possible." Our task was simple: evacuate Andre's mansion. The not-so-easy part was going to be staying alive.

The driver made good on our deal. We managed to make a forty-five minute drive in half the time. I threw a thick wad of bills at him as Leanne, Oliver, Caleb, and I dashed out of the car. Guests were still arriving, but the warm light from the mansion illuminated a room already full with people.

Grabbing the dark blue folds of fabric of my dress, I sprinted to the entrance, my friends quick on my heels. I tried not to think about the danger I was putting them in.

Bishopcourt loomed in front of us. Hundreds of glass bowls had been placed throughout the expansive yard, filled with water and floating candles. Light refracted off of the strangely beautiful decorations. Each tiny beacon of light reminded me that Andre had not seen natural light in nearly a millennia.

Classical music poured out of the front door. The crowds were thickest here. I jostled many guests as I approached the entrance.

Two large security personnel guarded the door. As

soon as they saw me, they parted to let me through but stopped my friends.

"They're with me," I yelled to the guards.

At that, they stepped aside and let my friends through. "Thanks!" I didn't pause, but pushed my way through the entrance.

I'd never realized it before, but most of the mansion was flammable, despite being built out of stone. The polished wood floors were covered with Persian rugs. Fabric insulated the walls, partially hidden by woven tapestries and oil paintings. Cloth drapes were pulled back from windows, and most of the furniture had wooden frames. Hundreds of candles perched on every open surface. I shuddered. Forget about the price on my head; this mansion was one wrong jostle away from going up in flames.

We'd decided earlier to split up, but it fell on me to direct my friends where to go. "Oliver and Leanne, take the stairs to the upper stories and start evacuating people from there. Caleb, you take the rooms to the left, and I'll take those to the right." Hopefully we'd have enough time to get everyone out before the fire broke out.

"Be safe Gabrielle!" Caleb shouted.

"You too!" I yelled back, but he had already vanished from sight. I hurried to the right, where the reception hall and ballroom were located. I'd yet to see Andre and hoped it would stay that way. Vaguely I could sense him, which probably meant he could sense me too. I'd have to do this quick.

Most of the ballroom was open space to make room for dancing. A string quartet played in the corner, playing classical music. Some couples danced in a rigid formation and others talked. I scanned the room for any type of platform. There was nothing to stand on but a few tables. They would have to do.

I pushed myself onto a table top, getting looks from those guests nearest me. "Excuse me!" I shouted from the table. Clusters of individuals near me turned to look. Others saw me standing and stopped to stare.

"Excuse me!" I shouted again. The room fell silent. Now I had everyone's attention. The guests however, were gawking at me as though I had grown a third eye. I guess I was breaking etiquette.

"A plot to burn down this building was discovered earlier tonight. You must all evacuate the mansion." There was murmuring, but no one moved. And then I felt Andre. He was moving swiftly towards this room. Frantic, I yelled, "Did you not hear me? Get the hell out of here unless you want to die!" The murmuring got louder and slowly the crowd began to move. A woman screamed as her companion grabbed her, and suddenly the room was bedlam.

I felt the current of energy spike, and instinctively I looked for Andre. He was making his way through the crowd over to me, and he did not look pleased.

"Gabrielle!" he shouted. I jumped down from the table and ran into the crowd, trying to hide myself.

The scary truth was that, while I knew my life was in danger and while I had killed before, I couldn't kill Andre. I couldn't even try, as cowardly as that was. I sent a silent apology to my father. At least no other lives but my own would be lost tonight.

A hand caught my arm. I cursed and looked up, expecting to see Andre. Instead, Theodore was smiling down at me.

"Exit's the other way," he said, "or are you not going to evacuate from the fire you've been raving about?"

I narrowed my eyes at him. "I was going to check some of the other rooms to make sure everyone has evacuated." I didn't want to tell him I was hiding from his boss.

"Good idea," he said. "I'll come with you."

I eyed him curiously, not sure whether he was being sincere or just toying with me. Either way, I needed to check the rooms on this side of the house, and I was willing to go along with it.

The ballroom we were in had two exits, one that led to the entrance hall, and another that led to a hallway and back rooms. We took this exit. I glanced behind me, but I could no longer see Andre and the current between us was fading. Theodore and I made our way to each of these back rooms.

Five minutes later we were done checking this wing of the house. All the rooms were empty except for the kitchen.

I leaned in the doorway. "Please evacuate the premises."

"Why?" one of the chefs asked.

"There's a fire hazard and the building's being emptied."

A grumbling chef and the surrounding help reluctantly filed out of the room.

Theodore watched me the entire time, giving me the creeps. I got the distinct impression he was taking note of my actions so that he'd have evidence when he turned me in.

"Why don't we check upstairs?" Theodore asked.

"Sure," I said, even though I knew Oliver and Leanne had probably evacuated them by now.

We peered into the first room. Empty. As we walked down the next, unease pooled in my stomach. Why hadn't Theodore brought me to Andre by now if he was going to turn me in, like he had the first time I met him? He followed me into the next room, a guest bedroom, which was also empty.

I turned to Theodore. "I think we should probably evacuate as well now," I said, hiding the unease from my voice. Unfortunately, I was still mostly human, so I couldn't hide the fear that slowly oozed from my pores.

Theodore closed the door, trapping us together in the room. He slung an arm around my shoulders and leaned in close. "What were you thinking? Coming here, making up lies about a nonexistent fire?"

"They are not lies." I tried to pull away from his

loose embrace.

Theodore pushed me forward. I fell to my knees and scrambled backwards, away from him. "How much do you know?" he asked.

I shook my head. "About what?"

Theodore stared intensely at me, trying to read my thoughts, and then he did. "You believe Andre is going to kill you." His voice held a note of disbelief.

I kept quiet. Theodore was still scrutinizing me. I had never seen the animalistic side of a vampire until Theodore turned those inquisitive, predatory eyes on me. Now I felt like lunch.

I saw a flicker of understanding pass across his eyes. "That was why you ran away from Andre in the banquet room." he said. He began to laugh hysterically. "You think he's after you?" My eyes widened. "Oh Gabrielle, you sweet, *stupid* girl. Do you realize you just initiated your own death?"

My breath caught in my throat as an awful thought was beginning to take shape.

"Ahhhh, you're finally getting it," he said. "Andre is not the one you need to fear. By the way, thank you for evacuating the entire building. No pesky witnesses or tragic heroes will hold this up."

Oh God. I'd misunderstood everything. Andre was innocent, and I was so scared of trusting him that I jumped to my hasty conclusion. Looking at Theodore now, I saw a guilty man.

He was right. I had put the final nail in my coffin—

so to speak. And now I was cornered in a windowless room, and the only way out was through the door Theodore guarded.

"Why?" I asked. That's what it really all came down to at this point. Answers.

Theodore curled his lip and stared at me. "Your parents took you to a seer when you were an infant," he said. "The seer looked into your future and predicted what you would become—a vampire.

"The problem is that she also saw something else—I assume you have heard of soulmates?"

I rolled my eyes. I was not that dumb.

Theodore continued. "The seer saw that you had a soulmate. She saw Andre."

Chapter 23

ANDRE AND I, soulmates. My heart fluttered, and then regret filled me. I'd pushed him away. And now I might die before I got the chance to apologize and try to fix things between us.

Theodore continued. "She also foresaw that, after your transition, you became queen, and under your reign, leagues of vampires were exterminated."

"What?" I would go on to commit genocide? The thought made me nauseous. Of course vampires did not exactly have clean consciences, but that I could be behind something so evil made my skin crawl. "That's impossible."

Before I could blink, Theodore had closed the space between us. I didn't see his fist move, but I heard my jaw crack as it connected with my face. Intense pain blossomed along my jawline, and I fell backwards. "Don't tell me what's impossible!" he yelled, his eyes wild.

His extreme mood swing was more startling than the sharp pain spreading across my face. And then, like flipping a light switch, his emotions were under control again.

"Why ... my father ..." It was hard to form words, and my jaw screamed as I spoke, but I had to know.

He smiled. "Not just your father. Your mother too."

I felt sick to my stomach. How poorly I misjudged the situation. He was responsible for my parents' deaths.

"And why? Because they knew. They knew and they protected you anyway. Them and Andre. But as you might already know, I can't exactly kill Andre if I'm trying to prevent the deaths of countless vampires. Killing him would mean killing *all* vampires. Well, all of them but one—you."

"I still don't understand—why kill my parents and me if the future is alterable?" I asked, careful about jostling my jaw. I knew that I would die before I was responsible for the mass extermination of vampires, regardless of their innocence.

"That is exactly what Andre said when he learned of the prophecy. He thought he could change your fate. So he forbid all vampires from making an attempt on your life. A true leader eliminates all threats to his people, but when it came to you, his soulmate, Andre put himself before his subjects. Coward. He has left the dirty work to me." With that, he grabbed my arm and yanked me to my feet.

He brought my neck to his mouth and bit down hard. I screamed as blood seeped down Theodore's chin and my neck. Theodore hissed an intake of breath. "Perhaps we can have a little fun before you die. You are truly an exquisite thing."

This was *not* how I was going die. Then Theodore's words sank in.

I thought back to when Andre and I practiced how to captivate prey. That barely contained monster had surfaced, the one that feasted off of sex and other dangerous things. The siren inside me.

I knew what I had to do—I'd just never consciously attempted it before. Theodore bent down to my neck and ran his tongue along the wound. I suppressed my horrified shiver and opened myself up to my unearthly heritage, which legend says men have died for.

I felt the warm rush of power as the siren took over.

"Theodore." I thought I had spoken his name, but it sounded more like an ethereal song. This voice could not be mine; I could never sound so seductive.

He stilled at my throat. Slowly he lifted his head up and looked into my eyes. I could almost see his wicked thoughts as he stared at me.

"You know you do not want to kill me ... yet." Again, I sang the words, my voice dripping of sex, an activity I *really* had no idea about.

Almost against his will he shook his head. "Stop it." He spoke through clenched teeth.

"I know what you want to do." I backed up towards the bed that loomed on the far side of the room and beckoned him to follow.

He gazed at me for a moment, his hands fisting as he tried to fight off the glamour. Gradually his hands slackened again as he became mesmerized, and then he began to follow me, no longer the feared predator.

I felt my control slipping. The siren in me wanted blood and sex, and she'd go all the way if she could. I put my hand to his chest, and pushed him partially onto the bed. His legs dangled over the mattress' edge, and I bent over him.

I slid my hands over his thighs and made a sound low in my throat. His eyes were too bright, and they watched me in awe. I moved my hands to his hair, running them through his wavy locks.

His own hands cupped my butt and then moved out to my hips. He pulled me closer, our lower bodies flush with one another.

Tantalizingly slow, I leaned towards him until my mouth hovered over his. There, I paused before pulling back.

I stared into his eyes. My heart pounded and my breathing was becoming erratic. "Now I am going to give you exactly what you deserve."

I slammed my knee as hard as I could into his

crotch—which, given my strength, was considerable.

He screamed like a wounded animal. I turned and sprinted down the hallway, towards the stairs. I looked behind me to see Theodore leaning on the doorway, painfully straightening up. Taking into account his superhuman speed, I had only bought myself a few precious seconds. I dashed around the banister, knocking over a few candles that rested on its edge. Behind me I smelled smoke as the rug caught on fire.

Crap, *I* was responsible for burning down the mansion?

"Gabrielle!" Theodore roared behind me. I flew down the steps, hoping I wouldn't trip in my stilettos. It would be a shame to escape death only to break my neck during my great escape.

Below me, I saw Andre fill the front doorway. "Gabrielle?"

"Andre—go!" I yelled. He could not die here too.

He looked quizzically at me, and then past me. "Theodore?"

Theodore must have registered that his time was up. He pulled out a gun. There was no hesitation. He looked down the barrel at me and fired. Almost instantaneously, something large and solid tackled me. My shoulder exploded as the bullet tore through muscle and tissue.

I shrieked as Andre and I hit the stairs, the pain causing my vision to cloud. Getting shot was just as unbearable the second time around as it was the first.

Andre stood up, his tux partially stained with my blood. An unholy fire blazed in his eyes as he stared Theodore down. The ground beneath us quaked. He was absolutely stunning and utterly terrifying.

I tried to sit up, but as soon as I moved, pain shot through my left side. I contented myself with watching everything sideways.

Slowly Andre walked the stairs towards Theodore. Each step he took shook the floor. Abandoned champagne flutes wobbled and china tinkled.

His eyes never strayed from Theodore, who stood paralyzed. "You tried to kill her," Andre's voice boomed.

The whole building shuddered at his words. Above me the giant chandelier rocked violently side to side. Dozens of candles toppled from their precarious perch, dropping from the chandelier and lighting the ancient rugs on fire. I took note that the fire was equally Andre's fault.

Theodore managed to stand his ground, although his hands quivered. "She's seen him, the devil. She's cursed."

I swallowed down my nausea. The devil? Was that who the man in the suit was? I couldn't imagine how Theodore knew this. Andre, however, didn't so much as pause at this revelation.

"She will lead to the death of us all." Theodore's words became rushed. "You could not protect your people, so I had to."

Poor Theodore misunderstood the situation. Even I could tell that Andre was beyond listening.

Andre's hair began to lift, as if caught by a breeze. "How dare you question my leadership!" he yelled. A violent tremor began at Andre's feet. The building's foundations groaned as it swept through the mansion, upending priceless sculptures and vases.

The enormous wrought iron chandelier shrieked, and with a awful snap, it began to fall.

"Gabrielle!" My head whipped around. Caleb ran towards me, cutting across the entrance hall. Dear God, the chandelier and he were on a collision course. He wasn't going to be able to clear the distance.

Time slowed. I began to move as the chandelier plunged towards him. My shoulder screamed as I forced myself up and my feet to move. But I wasn't fast enough.

"Caleb!"

He registered my alarm, his face changing from concern to confusion. And then the edge of the chandelier connected with his head. There was a sickening thump and Caleb's eyes rolled back as he fell limp.

The entire event happened in seconds, but it seemed to stretch on in my mind. Then time righted itself.

The chandelier hit the floor; its massive iron frame crumpled side tables and pulverized the wooden floorboards beneath. It sounded like hell had broken loose, and maybe it had. Debris rained over me from the fallout.

Above me Andre's anger still raged. "You took an oath to protect her, and instead you tried to kill her." The fire bloomed and spread in time to Andre's voice, licking up the thick drapery. "You betrayed the coven. You betrayed *me*!" Everywhere glass shattered.

Theodore started to back up, the whites of his eyes visible. Remembering the gun, he aimed it at me. Before his finger so much as caressed the trigger, the gun flew from his hand.

Horror bloomed on Theodore's usually confident face as he looked at his empty hand. Apparently he hadn't fully realized the extent of Andre's power either. Theodore turned to run.

"No," Andre ordered. The doors along the hallway slammed shut. Andre wrapped his hand around one of the banister rails and ripped it away from the staircase.

Theodore staggered. "No, not that." He began to beg. "Please Andre, have mercy."

Andre grabbed Theodore's hair and pulled his head backward, exposing his neck.

"Please, please, please," Theodore said, over and over again.

"There is no mercy for traitors." Andre lifted the stake and, in one clean stroke, thrust it through Theodore's heart. Above the roaring of the fire, I heard screams coming from outside.

My stomach roiled. Andre dropped Theodore's

body and walked back down the stairs. His rage had not subsided. With every step he took the fire expanded, until I was uncomfortably hot.

He approached me, and I tried to move away from him. Uncaring, he scooped me up, and I screamed as he jostled my shoulder. I was pressed against Andre's bloody tux, soaked with my blood and now Theodore's.

Andre didn't so much as pause as we passed Caleb. We were leaving without him. "Wait, we have to get Caleb." Andre ignored me. "Andre, did you hear me? Put me down."

"No." We crossed the mansion's threshold then were outside. I breathed in the crisp evening air. People gathered in clusters, some whispering to each other as they watched us, others crying.

Here and there I noticed strange piles of singed clothing. And then an unsettling thought crept up on me. If Andre's death would kill everyone he'd ever changed, could Theodore's death kill the vampires he'd created too?

"Oh God ..." But Andre must've known this. He must have known that killing Theodore would indirectly kill so many others. But if he knew ... My stomach churned. If he knew, then his actions were horrific.

"Put me down!"

"No," he said. His voice had lost its otherworldly anger. "You may hate me, but I will not let you go back inside." Andre finally met my gaze, and he looked normal again. A droplet of blood snaked from his eye. It took me a moment to realize it was a tear. "I cannot let you die."

He was not going to let me save my friend. He'd hold me back and let Caleb die—if he wasn't dead already. I couldn't let that happen.

For a second time that evening I coaxed the sinister siren to the surface. I opened myself up and let my power take over. My skin began to glow lightly.

Andre's eyes widened when he realized what I was doing. But it was already too late. "Put me down." Once again my voice was not my own.

Andre hesitated.

I brushed a piece of hair away from his face. "Put me down," I repeated, my voice melodic. His jaw clenched and unclenched. Slowly, so slowly, he let me down. I could tell he was trying to fight it, but even he could be swayed.

As soon as my feet touched the ground, I began to run, keeping my injured arm close to my body. I didn't know how much time I'd have before he regained full control of his actions.

My skin was still glowing, and I noticed individuals approaching me as the siren pulled them in.

Although only a minute had passed since I was last inside, the mansion was now largely consumed by flames. I hesitated only briefly before plunging in. Once inside, smoke obscured my vision, and my eyes teared up almost immediately. I made my way through the smoke to the chandelier. Next to it was my fallen friend.

Caleb lay so still that I was convinced he was dead. I knelt down and felt for a pulse. It was there, very weak but there nonetheless. I almost collapsed with relief.

I hooked my arms underneath his. A wave of nausea passed over me as I forced my injured shoulder to support Caleb's weight. I took in a deep breath, steadied myself, and pulled him to his feet. Lifting him was effortless, but I screamed from the intense pain shooting through my arm as I moved it. He moaned, slowly coming to, and I almost cried out my relief.

"Gabrielle?" He began to cough.

"Hey sleepyhead, not the best place for a nap!" I had to yell to be heard above the fire.

He smiled then winced and rubbed his head.

"We need to get out of here!"

I let him lean on me as I walked us through the haze and back to the mansion's main entrance. As soon as I could see it, however, I knew there was no way of getting out. The large oak doors were engulfed in flames, turning our escape into a wall of fire. My heart dropped. We were trapped in a burning house.

"We're going to have to figure out another exit," I said.

This was beginning to feel like déjà vu; I had lived through one fire already.

That's it.

"Persecution tunnels," I said.

"What?"

"Can you walk?" I asked him.

Slowly he nodded. "I think so."

"Good. We need to head to the kitchen. There should be a tunnel beyond."

I was desperately hoping that Bishopcourt was somewhat similar to my childhood home. If the pantry connected to the kitchen contained a wine cellar, then it would be the perfect place to put a persecution tunnel. If it didn't ... I refused to think about the alternative.

Something in the distance crashed, and I began to walk us towards the east wing.

Caleb paused to catch his breath, leading to another coughing fit. Meanwhile my eyes were tearing up from the heat. Time was quickly running out for the two of us.

The walls and ceiling of the hallway off of the main entrance were on fire, but luckily they were wide and high enough to pass through mostly unscathed. I sent up a silent prayer that the floor here was marble.

We were almost to the other end of the hall when I heard a wall behind us crash.

"Can you run?" I asked Caleb.

"No, I don't think so."

"Hmmm." Could I carry him and get us out in time?

"But I might be able to shapeshift."

"Shapeshift?"

He let out a shaky cough, reminding me how injured he was. "Change into an animal. Something you could hold so I don't slow you down."

I nodded. "Let's try that." It was the best idea we had. If he changed, I could use my supernatural speed, increasing our chances of survival.

Caleb closed his eyes and exhaled. His skin rippled, and he began to shrink and thin. Scales formed, replacing skin. His body curved and coiled until he was nothing more than a garden snake sitting amongst his crumpled clothing.

I repressed a shudder. I'd never been a big fan of snakes, and up until now I'd never held one. I bent down and hurriedly picked Caleb up; the ground must be scalding. He slithered up my injured arm, and I bit back a scream as he coiled himself around it.

After he was securely wrapped around my arm, I dashed down the hallway and turned left. The fire had only tentatively made its way down this hall. The third door on the left was the kitchen, and I sprinted through.

Inside, the walls were beginning to smoke, and the exposed beams on the ceiling had caught fire. At the back of the room the door to the pantry was still untouched by the flames. Above me there was a groan, and a flaming beam fell between the pantry door and me.

I'd have to jump over the beam. I looked down at

my long dress and heels. If I went through that pantry and there was no connected cellar, I might not be able to get us out of here. *Why had I not chosen a window when I had the chance?*

I ripped more than half my skirt off and wound the excess material around my free arm. I backed up and took a running jump over the beam, singeing myself as I leapt over it.

I got up on the other side and assessed the pantry door. Like all doors, it had a metal handle. Using the material wrapped around my arm as a buffer, I opened the door and dashed inside. At the back of the pantry there was a rectangle cut into the floor. *A cellar door.* I wanted to cry in relief. I hadn't doomed us. Someone had propped it open, presumably to bring out wines stored below.

I descended the stairs and closed the hatch above us. Smoke trickled in through the door's cracks at an alarming rate. We weren't out of danger yet.

Shelves and shelves of wines covered the walls of the cavernous cellar. Andre's anger had broken most of the bottles. I didn't stop to ponder just how priceless each remaining one was. I began toppling shelves. Hundreds of broken and intact glass bottles shattered as the racks crashed to the floor. One down. Two down. Three down. I'd only cleared one of the four walls. And yet no persecution tunnel.

I began coughing, choking on the smoke that was rapidly filling up the cellar. I was running out of time and shelves. I pushed over another shelf on the adjacent wall. There was nothing but solid earth behind it. I screamed out in frustration. The cellar was too big; there wasn't enough time to bring down all the wine racks that covered the walls.

I rubbed my temples. Think, *think*. But I couldn't think; if I could, Caleb and I would have been outside long before now. I was running on adrenaline alone.

Breathing in and out, I steadied myself. I caught the faintest whiff of grass and felt the cool brush of an almost imperceptible breeze. My head snapped up. The breeze came from the wall opposite me.

Please let this be it. I walked over and began yanking down the shelves.

And there it was. Behind one of the shelves was a hollow space.

Stepping over the broken shelves, I led us down the pitch-black tunnel. Even with my good night vision I had to grope a bit to get my bearings.

It felt like an eternity before I reached the end of the tunnel. By the time I arrived, my arm was throbbing and Caleb's hold was loosening. I felt along the damp walls, trying to find the door that led out. My hand bumped into a ladder.

Tentatively I tested it. When it didn't collapse under my weight, I began climbing.

My head hit wood, and raising my good arm, I pushed against it. The damp wood groaned in protest, and I redoubled my effort. Above me I heard the sound of snapping roots as I displaced the plants that had grown above the hidden door. With a final push, the wooden door gave, and moonlight streamed down on me.

I climbed out and collapsed onto the ground, and Caleb uncoiled himself. His scales began to ripple, and slowly he morphed back into his natural form. Under normal circumstances I would've blushed when I realized I was looking at Caleb's naked backside. But now, having nearly escaped death a few times, propriety was the last thing on my mind.

He dry heaved a few times before flopping down next to me. The door had led us out to the back of the property, so close to the ocean that I could smell the musty sea. In the distance we could see the fire department containing the fire. Luckily it hadn't spread to the surrounding greenery.

"Thanks for saving my life," Caleb said softly.

I looked at the stars, happy to be alive. "Thanks for coming tonight and helping me save mine."

Epilogue

One Month Later

I TUGGED MY dark green dress down and looked at my date. Caleb and Rodrigo, the Brazilian werewolf Oliver had invited to the Autumn Ball, were discussing shapeshifting. When he noticed me staring, Caleb flashed me a secret smile, his blue eyes glittering with something more than friendship. I returned the smile. My stomach didn't flutter like it probably should have, but at least Caleb was a safe, healthy choice as far as dates went.

I tried not to think about the man I wished were here instead. After trying and failing to convince myself for the last month that my feelings for Andre were gone, I'd settled on the truth: I loved him, but his actions during the night of the fire had terrified me. Despite being his soulmate—something I was having a hard time accepting—I wasn't sure I could be with someone who'd knowingly damned dozens of his own people in order to save me. That sort of devotion was a little too intense—and volatile—for my taste.

It didn't, however, mean that I could get over him. Nor did it stop me from staring at his number in my weaker moments, imagining what it would be like to bring things back to the way they were.

"Hey gorgeous," Oliver came up behind me. "Isn't Rodrigo delicious?" he asked. He saw my troubled face. "Don't tell me you're thinking about *him* again?"

"Oliver! I—"

"I'm not asking you to defend yourself. Just make a decision and move on."

"I have, only it's a bit hard considering he's my *soulmate*," I snapped.

"Is everything okay?" Caleb had wandered over and was now looking between Oliver and me.

"Everything's fine," I said, smiling reassuringly.

"Good." Caleb tucked a strand of my hair behind my ear, his fingers lingering, before he pulled me into a hug. Over his shoulder I saw Oliver shaking his head.

"Congratulations again—about joining the Politia," Caleb whispered into my ear.

A member of the department had visited me while Caleb and I were still in the hospital and offered me a position on the secret supernatural force. Apparently they'd been scouting me for weeks, and my role in the deaths of dozens of vampires and the rescue of Caleb—who the Politia was grooming to become their star enforcer—had convinced them of my qualifications.

"Thanks," I whispered back into his ear. He'd made it sound like an honor, but I'd only reluctantly accepted the offer, using the logic of keeping your friends close and your enemies closer. I didn't trust the Politia. The supernatural community didn't like vampires, and the Politia represented and enforced the community's values. But perhaps getting to know me would change their minds.

I moved my lips away from Caleb's ear and made the mistake of breathing in. The heady smell of his blood, pulsing just under the skin of his neck, caught me off guard, and I felt my canines extend. I pulled back quickly and turned away from him.

"I think I need some fresh air," I said, my back to him.

"Is everything alright?"

"Yes, yes," I mumbled, already moving away from him. "I'll be right back."

Thankfully he didn't try to follow me as I left Peel's ballroom and walked outside. The fierce wind grabbed at my hair and my gown, beckoning me towards the edge of the castle grounds. I leaned against the ancient stone wall, which ran the perimeter of the school. A hundred feet below, the surf crashed onto the rocks.

"It would be so easy to jump," a voice beside me said. "A swift fall and a quick death. Hundreds of students have done it over the centuries."

My head whipped to my side, but no one was there. I looked around me. Thirty feet away the man in a suit leaned against the castle wall, blending into the shadows.

I put a hand to my chest. I hadn't seen him since the night he'd taken me.

"What, thought I was gone? Not after the night we spent together." He winked at me. I felt sick to my stomach; I still didn't know what had happened to me that night.

"I know who you are," I said. That much Theodore had helped me with. The man in the suit wasn't a figment of my imagination. No, it was much worse. He was the devil, Lucifer, the most beautiful angel who'd fallen from heaven.

"I guess the jig's up." He pouted. "And I was having so much fun convincing you that you were insane."

My hands were shaking from his nearness, and I bit the inside of my cheek to hold back the scream that wanted to bubble to the surface. The delicate skin tore and I tasted blood.

"Having problems these days with your ... cravings?" he asked.

"Of course not," I said, my elongated canines contradicting me. Not to mention that I was no longer on speaking terms with my mentor, the one person who might be able to help me control my urges.

"You know, it seems interesting to me that the Politia still haven't found the hired hitmen who tried to kill you."

"They're working on it," I said, doubt creeping into my voice. Somehow he knew my fears and exploited them.

"Of your attackers, I especially find the shapeshifter interesting. Did you know that's a hereditary ability? Would be awfully problematic if your boyfriend's father was the one who tried to murder you."

"He's not my boyfriend."

"Oh right. That title belongs to Andre, the cold-blooded killer. Pass along my thanks. I had many new arrivals that night."

"Just leave me the hell alone," I said. I began walking back towards the ballroom.

"Never." His voice was a whisper in my ear. "Enjoy your night. I'll be watching you."

To Be Continued ...

Keep a lookout for the sequel:

The Coveted

Coming in 2014

LAURA THALASSA LIVES in Santa Barbara, California with her boyfriend, Daniel Ricchiazzi. *The Unearthly* is her debut novel. When not writing, you can find her at www.laurathalassa.blogspot.com

Acknowledgements

FIRST AND FOREMOST, this book would not have existed without the love and encouragement of Daniel Ricchiazzi. You inspired me to write, but more than that, you inspired me to be the greatest version of myself that I could. Thank you for all that you are; I love you immensely.

Alison Lanier, now it's your turn to write a book! You were my first writing partner as well as best friend, and it's you who nurtured my early love of writing and never laughed at my half-baked stories (well, at least not all that much). Most of the humor in this book has some root in our adventures together. Thank you for always being there, just a phone call away, and accepting me just the way I am.

Dad, since I was a kid you've been the biggest supporter of my writing. I'll never forget the walks we'd go on, the topic of conversation somehow always coming back to writing. I'm so glad you relentlessly encouraged me.

Grandpa Hall, you were one of the first people to point out to me that I might actually be a half decent writer. But more than that, you encouraged me to work at it. Thank you—I don't plan on stopping anytime soon!

To Sunniva, thank you so much for the laughs, edits, and inspiring messages. Get your book out there so that our books can be friends! By the way, I'm still convinced that you'd make an awesome editor!

I owe a huge thanks to my mom, who's the salt of the earth. You are the strongest woman I know, and I hope to be like you one day. Thank you for always coming up with creative solutions to problems, embracing my weirdness (because we all know who I inherited that trait from!), and geeking out with me over books.

To Teresa, you always give me more than I deserve and you are always the first person I call when calamity strikes. Thank you for never forgetting a birthday and always putting in the extra effort. As scatterbrained as I am, I do notice, and it means the world to me.

To Grace and Michael, I couldn't ask for better siblings if I picked them myself. I love you to pieces my little string bean; you have the best personality out there. And Mike, thanks for always keeping things real ... or at least real interesting.

Lastly, to Dan's parents, you are both some of the kindest, most genuinely caring people I know. Thanks for rooting for me and raising the most wonderful son a girl could ask for!